THE COMPUTER ROOM

STORIES

BY

EMMA

ENSLEY

LOBLOLLY
PRESS

2025

LOBLOLLY✸PRESS

Published by Loblolly Press
loblollypress.com
Asheville, NC

Cover design by Emma Ensley
Interior design by Andrew Mack
Editorial support from Mara K. Bell

Instagram: @loblolly_press
Newsletter: loblollypress.substack.com

Paperback ISBN: 979-8-9900730-5-0
Ebook ISBN: 979-8-9900730-6-7
Printed in the United States of America
Library of Congress Control Number: 2025943187

First Printing, September 2025

CONTENTS

THE COMPUTER ROOM

THICK FISH

Daisy's brother and his two friends named their band Thick Fish. They got the name by just opening the dictionary up to two random words. Said that's how all the best bands did it. It was catchy enough, but I think they could have done the whole thing again. Maybe tried to land on something better.

We used to watch Thick Fish play, Daisy and I. We would sit on her brother's bed, getting our eardrums blasted off by the speakers while they covered a Green Day song. Or sang one of their own. Or tried to learn Radiohead. Daisy's brother had bangs that covered his eyes when he played guitar. All his friends had that same floppy hair that formed greasy little ropes at the ends. I was grossed out, but I also wanted to reach out and feel it.

Daisy's house was always messy. It smelled like their five pets, who ran in and out of the house of their own volition. They'd keep the windows open in the summer, because there was no AC, and the smell of cigarettes would float in from the neighbor's house. We could always hear him yelling about something unimportant.

I liked watching Thick Fish practice because it made me feel like I was in some behind-the-scenes music documentary on VH1. Like I was watching something really special happen. It made me think that, maybe someday, I'd be interviewed about Thick Fish's early days. And I could say something like "I knew they were going to make it" or "they always had that special something". I'd be a real Thick Fish expert.

I think it annoyed Daisy that her brother always had his friends over to play such loud music. Since they shared a wall, she said it was hard to watch the TV in her room. She couldn't play *The Sims* with the sound on. She couldn't practice her own keyboard, which she had just gotten last Christmas and that lit up when she pressed different keys. She never watched them practice if I wasn't over to convince her.

Daisy's room was messier than the whole rest of the house. I'd never seen it clean. She kept her clothes in piles on the floor and piles on her bed. She scooted the clothing mountains over when it was time to sleep. Sometimes just kicking one a little bit with her leg was enough. She kept plates and cups on her bedside table, like a museum. Ancient artifacts, revealing Daisy only ate buttered noodles and only drank Coca-Cola.

I liked spending weekend nights at Daisy's house because we could walk to the park across the street and play monkey bars with her next-door neighbors, Heather and Brooke. Heather and Brooke were younger than us and went to a different school. They lived with their dad who always had his shirt off and was the reason Daisy's house smelled like cigarettes. Their accents were thicker than mine.

Brooke and Heather liked to take the bottom of their tank tops and flip them through the neck of their shirt, pulling the hem down so that the whole shirt looked like a bra and your belly showed. They taught me how to do it and I wore my shirt like that every time we hung from the monkey bars. I figured my belly was going to show anyway in that position.

I learned to like cold pizza at Daisy's house; we'd eat it for breakfast. I learned to like The Red Hot Chili Peppers. And Green Day. Any song that Thick Fish played. I even learned to like Howard Stern, which was what we'd watch late at night, often falling asleep cuddled against Daisy's piles of tank tops—stretched out from our belly reveals. Daisy never turned her TV off; she only turned the volume down.

"My brother's home from school for two weeks, he got suspended," Daisy said to me one night on the swing set at the park. I had my tank top flipped up and was straddling the swing so I could face Daisy, who sat the same way on the other one. "He had weed in his pocket."

"Woah." I said it, quietly, just in case. "Are your parents mad?"

"I don't think so," Daisy said with a sigh. She dug the heels of her plastic, chunky sandals into the rocks beneath us.

Daisy's mom was a special education teacher, and her dad did landscaping. He wasn't around much and the only thing I knew about him was that he had a dulcimer, wedged between some boxes in their computer room. I thought it was such a pretty instrument. I'd play hymns on it, hitting the strings with Daisy and flipping through the sheet music, pretending that we knew what any of it meant. That must be where her brother got it—his musical genius.

Daisy put her pinky out, confidently, looking for a promise. "Let's never do drugs."

This was an easy promise for me to make. I didn't know anybody who smoked weed. I didn't even know where you'd find it or what it felt like. I only knew about drugs from *Degrassi* and the fifth-grade D.A.R.E. program.

"Promise," I said to Daisy, anyway.

Daisy had a crush on the one boy at school in the drama club and despite this new information, I had a crush on Daisy's brother. Daisy was allowed to talk about her crush as much as she wanted but I kept mine a secret. We planned out Daisy and her crush's future children's names—first and middle. We bought wedding magazines from the grocery store and cut out the white dresses that she liked, and the bridesmaids' dresses that I liked. Sometimes we would cut the magazines right in the center of Daisy's bed and leave the scraps where they fell—pushing them into a pile at our feet when it was time to go to bed.

Daisy's brother was at home a lot more, since the suspension, and his band mates weren't allowed to come over. He kept his bedroom door closed and he played the same riff from *Jesus of Suburbia* over and over into his amp. I could hear him cuss when he messed up.

Heather and Brooke knocked on the door and asked Daisy and me to go to the park and hang upside down with them.

"Mom!" Daisy yelled to the back of the house. "We're going to the park!" Daisy's mom emerged from her bedroom, a room I'd never seen before, and touched Daisy gently on the shoulder.

"Ok," She sighed. She always seemed exhausted. "Take your brother."

"Mom, no," Daisy groaned.

"At least ask him. He needs to get out of the house."

Daisy rolled her eyes and shuffled her way to her brother's door.

"Hey," she yelled, instead of knocking, and opened the door before there was even a response.

"What the fuck, Daisy." His amp rang out as he set his guitar down. Like an alarm.

"We're going to the park." She rolled her eyes. "Wanna come?"

Surprisingly, he slipped on his sneakers and followed us out the door.

Clouds hung low in the sky, stretched-out like cotton balls. There was music playing down the street and the air smelled like hot dogs over a barbecue. Now and again a baby would shriek or giggle, both noises sounding pretty much the same.

The park was empty and Heather and Brooke took turns doing round-offs in the grass, their feet coming together in the air for one magical moment before they popped back upright, hands to the sky.

They showed us a cheer they'd learned from watching the older girls at the football games. "Purple, purple! Gold, gold!" They shouted in thick voices, clapping their hands together in sharp, loud cups.

Daisy's brother did a pull-up on the monkey bars and hoisted his whole body to the top, until he was perched high above us all. He shook his stringy hair out of his face and gazed in the distance, like his mind was somewhere else. I wanted to sit next to him, but I knew my arms were too weak. I couldn't do that same maneuver. So I acted like I didn't notice him, either.

I thought about saying that I hate cheerleaders, even though I wasn't sure if that was true. I wanted him to know that Daisy and me didn't practice tumbling at the park and that I mostly ignored the chants I heard from the bleachers when my parents took me to football games on Friday nights. I wanted him to see me as someone more like him and less like anyone else.

"Stop being weird," Daisy said, flicking the side of my shoulder. "You're being so quiet."

"Sorry," I mumbled, rubbing the spot on my arm.

Daisy's brother laid back on the top of the monkey bars, with his arms spread out, all Christ-like. *Jesus of Suburbia.*

I didn't dare flip my shirt.

IS ANY1 A CHRISTIAN???

Seemed like everyone in Tess's tiny town was obsessed with God. All the kids in her middle school were in the same youth group and they talked about church lock-ins and Sunday night gatherings like they were the social events of the year. There would always be some kids that started "going out" from those lock-ins. People even kissed at them. They all had Bible verses in their away messages.

Tess asked her mom if she could go on the big middle school mission trip to Jamaica. Her best friend, Grace, was going and Tess didn't want to spend her whole spring break alone at home. She wanted to be at the beach with all the other godly kids, playing Spin the Bottle in the back of the church van and singing along to those pretty acoustic songs.

Her mom scoffed at her request. "If you really want to help, there are plenty of people to help right here."

Tess could watch whatever she wanted on TV, but Grace was only allowed to see certain things. Grace's parents liked the show *7th Heaven* because the dad was a preacher and because it had something called "family values," so they let her watch as much of it as she wanted.

Tess and Grace would spend hours marathoning the show and eating pepperonis from the package while lying on their stomachs. Tess hadn't been to high school yet and felt a rush of excitement and fear, watching the struggles that might come her way. Would she get offered drugs someday and have to say no? Be tempted by premarital sex? She learned what cutting was when the middle daughter, Lucy, walked in on her friend, all bloodied in the bathroom.

Tess was allowed to go on the family computer for one hour every night after dinner and she usually used the hour to talk to Grace on AIM or to feed her Neopets. But once Grace left for Jamaica, she started looking up pictures of the *7th Heaven* cast. She scrolled through, imagining what it would be like to have this big, close family—someone older around to learn things from. Tess didn't have any siblings, she only had Grace.

The photos led her to TheWB.com, the website for the network that put all the new episodes out. There were forums for every show on the air; One Tree Hill, Summerland, Smallville. Tess clicked on the *7th Heaven* forum and found a seemingly endless number of threads.

Bush or Kerry??

is any1 a christian????

how old was ruthie when she got her first boyfriend?

thoughts about Simon and the STD

coke pepsi or dr pepper?

im New~

if u were stuck on a deserted island which guy off
7th heaven would u want to save u

terri schiavo

happy bday Jessica Biel!!!

At the top sat a pinned folder for something called "Fan Fiction." Intrigued, she clicked inside and discovered page after page of people writing their own episodes and stories. She found a post from someone named DreamStreetFan89 and decided it must be the best one, the best Fan Fiction, with 63 pages of replies and a little flame icon next to it. In this person's re-imagining, we were several years into the future and Lucy was married with children of her own— one of whom was just beginning middle school. This daughter was the focus. It was Lucy's kid, now tempted by the evils of teenage-hood. DreamStreetFan89 released a new segment every week, just like the real show.

When Tess lay in bed that night, long after her hour was up, she could still see the pages of flashing flame icons. DreamStreetFan89's story was good, but she wondered if she could do better.

Over spring break, while all the other kids were off in Jamaica praising the Lord and taking photos for MySpace, she got to work.

Tess focused her story in the present world of *7th Heaven*, choosing to take a more realistic approach. First, she wrote a couple of scenes that were mostly just the siblings interacting with each other, trying to get a good feel for how they talked. Having siblings was her favorite thing to imagine.

A house full of conversation and activity—it seemed so exciting. She clicked NEW POST, copy-and-pasted over the story from her Word document, and held her breath as she pressed send.

She refreshed the page, watching her post quickly sink below more active threads. She tried not to get discouraged, leaning back into the computer chair, waiting. When she hit refresh again, she had a reply from someone named heavennoseven. "keep going!" they said. And so, she did.

Tess started writing *7th Heaven* Fan Fiction every day, waking up and writing in her notebook so she could save her precious computer hour for transcribing. She added heavennoseven, whose real name was Julie, on AIM where they would talk about her writing. Julie would give her critiques and they would talk about her favorite lines. She would message Tess, urging her to post, if she hadn't yet that day.

"Mom, do we have a Bible?" Tess asked one night over dinner. Her mom looked up from her plate of spaghetti but didn't answer. There were a lot of things Tess could get away with imagining—what sisters fought about, what high school boys might say in the hallway. But she couldn't make up Bible passages or things about Jesus. Everyone would know if she tried that. She had to be accurate.

"I think I have one of your grandmother's somewhere." Tess could tell her mom was trying to be careful. "Why?"

"Research, mainly."

Tess skimmed through Genesis in bed that night, underlining.

Beyond Adam and Eve, a story she already knew, the Book of Genesis had mostly men's names. Enoch, father of Kenan, father of Mahalalel, father of Jared, on and on and on for pages. It was incredibly boring.

She flipped ahead to the Book of Job, wondering what kind of occupations people even had back then. She read about the angels and the Lord having a conversation with Satan, the messenger visiting Job and telling him awful things. How he shaved his head and got naked, as a reaction, screaming about why bad things happen to good people. Tess closed the book. She had her next idea.

In the morning, Tess sat with her journal and wrote a tale about the youngest Camden daughter, Ruthie. Ruthie was receiving secret poems in her locker. At first, they were kind of romantic and sweet, but slowly they turned mean.

> *Roses are red, violets are blue*
> *All of your friends, secretly hate you*

Ruthie acted like she didn't care but she began to feel super weird about the whole thing. She thought about it all day. Do her friends really hate her? More poems showed up and she started to think it must be true. Everyone probably hated her.

> *Roses are red, violets are blue*
> *Your curly hair, needs a shampoo*

Ruthie crumpled up the note and asked her friend, "Is my hair okay?" But her friend didn't say anything.

"Does it look gross?" Still nothing. Ruthie got scared and ran home super fast.

When she got home, her sister yelled "Ruthie!" but Ruthie just threw her backpack down and ignored her.

She ran upstairs and slammed the bathroom door and locked it. Her brother Simon's electric razor was on the counter. Ruthie looked in the mirror and smiled. She turned on the razor and it buzzed in her hand. Then she cut off all her curly black hair. It was all over her clothes. She took off her clothes and got in the shower. The warm water felt weird on her head.

⧗

tessButterfly27: what do you think?

heavennoseven: woah

heavennoseven: it's pretty intense

tessButterfly27: it's based on the story of job

heavennoseven: what job?

tessButterfly27: job from the bible

tessButterfly27: who got mad at god and shaved his head

heavennoseven: oh

heavennoseven: ok yea, I didn't get that

tessButterfly27: you don't like it?

heavennoseven: i just don't think ruthie would really do that, is all

Tess stopped showing Julie her writing before she posted it. heavennoseven clearly did not understand.

Tess read a new book of the Bible every night and ended each of her posts with a verse from that book.

Simon Camden, as a metaphor for Judas, turning his dad in for an expired parking ticket. *How much will you pay me to betray Jesus to you? Matthew 26:14.*

Mary Camden, as a metaphor for Delilah, tricking her boyfriend into proposing. *With such nagging she prodded him day after day until he was tired to death. Judges 16.*

Tess didn't really enjoy reading the Bible, nor did she understand it very much, but she loved watching her replies go up from 30 to 50 to 80.

`thx for writing ur stories, i don't know what i'd do without them,` MaryCamdennFan wrote under Tess's latest post.

angel05 said, `i get so excited for these everyday!!` and SimCecillia wrote `ur such a good writer and christian xo.`

Tess had barely thought about Grace or the mission trip all week. She only cared about the flame icon next to her name, ever-present, ever-burning.

Grace got home from Jamaica on Sunday night, just in time for school to start back the next day. Her mom brought her to Tess's house, on the way home, so she could give her a souvenir.

"I got you this," Grace said, holding out a keychain with Tess's name on it. "I know that sometimes they don't have your name."

Tess took it and ran her finger over the shiny, ocean-colored plastic. "Thanks."

Grace was freshly tanned, with freckles all over her face and a pink and blue hair wrap that hung from somewhere behind her left earlobe. She had on a bright green, too large, t-shirt that said *Building Hope. Youth Mission Team.*

"How was the trip?"

They sat in the computer room, sipping on Dr. Peppers.

"Good! Josh and Emily are going out. They held hands the whole time on the airplane. It was so cute." Grace touched her hair wrap, gently swirling it around her finger. Tess looked away, trying her best to hide her jealousy. She hadn't noticed there were beads on it, too. "And Tyler accepted Jesus into his heart, in front of everyone." She scratched at her peeling, sunburnt forearm. "Allie has a crush on him now. Now that he's not going to hell." Grace paused.

"Anyway, what did you do all break?"

Tess glanced at her computer, still open to TheWB.com on her pages of replies. She thought about her grandmother's old Bible, down the hall in her bedroom, still smelling of fresh highlighter, and wondered if Grace and the others read the Bible while they were in Jamaica or if the point was to get a tan and a boyfriend.

Tess shrugged and squeezed the keychain in her hand until it left a mark in her palm. "Not much," she said, the words sticky in her soda-stained mouth. "Can I show you something?"

BABYLAND

Blair lifts her shirt over her head in the front seat of her Volvo and fumbles around in the back for her scrubs. She's hungover and prays it's not obvious, smoothing out her greasy blonde hair, messy from the shirt swap. Her phone buzzes. Nurse Vicky.

You're coming in? Birthday party today.

"Fuck," Blair mutters, turning off her car with one hand and slipping a shoe on with the other. She'd almost forgotten. Birthday parties always require extra setup.

She weaves through the parking lot, patting the last giant, ceramic Cabbage Patch head for luck.

"Hey, Emilio," she says, passing by the front desk, twirling her keys around her finger. Emilio is the only Babyland General employee remotely close to her age and the best source of gossip. He's always got a story about some crazy field party or secretly hooking up with football players.

He looks up, eyebrows arched. He's been here for an hour already. "You're late again."

She turns and puts a finger over her mouth before heading to the back to put on her stethoscope and name tag.

"Finally." Nurse Vicki stands. "Let's go."

Blair started working at Babyland General early in the summer when all her friends began leaving for college. There aren't a ton of employment options in her tiny North Georgia town. There's the Bojangles down the street and the Party City that she worked at a few summers back. Growing up, her mom always told her she could be a doctor. This was the closest she would get.

Nurse Vicki reaches into a cabinet and pulls out the Cabbage Patch-themed paper napkins and plates as she briefs Blair. "Marley. Turning six today."

Babyland sees hundreds of kids daily, but birthday parties get special treatment: back room access, snacks, punch, and the opportunity to be first in line to adopt the Cabbage Patch doll born that day. Eighty-five dollars for some beady-eyed baby with yarn for hair. Money down the drain.

Blair hates kids. She never wanted any of her own and when she was a junior in high school and saw the white stick in her palm grow a little pink line, she took all her Party City money and got her brother to drive her 45 minutes down the road to Atlanta.

"I can't believe they're not allowed to teach us about sex in school, but there's a whole tourist attraction telling kids that babies come from tree roots," Emilio once said to her, when they were closing together after a particularly busy day. He was straightening up some cowboy-themed dolls on the shelf. "I can't wait to get out of here."

Blair didn't know if he meant Babyland General or North Georgia altogether. She could see him in downtown Atlanta in some sky rise apartment holding a martini. Maybe even New York City performing on Broadway.

"Marley," Blair repeats, assuredly to Nurse Vicki, setting the napkins down at each tiny spot on the table.

Marley and six of her friends arrive in smock dresses with bows in their hair. They are a loud bunch, and the shrieks they make when they pick a doll off the shelf make Blair's headache worsen.

Nurse Vicki doesn't seem to mind. Blair watches as she ushers them around the store, gently guiding their sticky hands away from the places they aren't supposed to be and complimenting their shoes and bracelets.

"You look six years old today," Nurse Vicki says gently to Marley, whose eyes light up.

"I *am* six years old today!"

"There's a birth in ten minutes at Mother Cabbage!" Emilio says, theatrically, over the loudspeaker. "I repeat, dilation is eight leaves, all staff on standby."

"Births" happen once an hour, on the hour, and are the highlight of most people's trip to Babyland General. By this point, Blair knew the script by heart, but she rarely performed the births, choosing instead to be a support from the sidelines.

During a "birth," a nurse stands at "Mother Cabbage" —a giant tree housing fifty Cabbage Patch babies in its roots. The tree's branches are decorated with several little fairies, tied to twinkle lights, which flash different colors throughout the show. Surrounded by bald heads peeking out from cabbage leaves, the nurse guides the tree through labor.

Children guess if the baby is going to be a boy or a girl by chanting "pink, pink, pink" or "blue, blue, blue", something Emilio once described as "antiquated and disgustingly binary."

The tree receives a shot of "Imagicillin" for pain, a term that's become a running joke between the employees. "Time for my Imagicillin" nurses say, before heading to the Mexican restaurant down the road for half-off margaritas.

On the nurse's cue, the crowd yells "Push!" A floppy doll with an oversized head emerges from the leaves, held up high like Simba.

Marley loves it. She claps and cheers and holds her hands to her face in excitement as the baby crowns. "My baby, mama!" She says, keeping her eyes ahead, grabbing at her mom's skirt. Her mom is watching through an iPhone screen. "Mama, my baby."

"I'm too hungover for this," Blair says out of the corner of her mouth to Emilio, who has walked up beside her in the back corner. He smiles. Mother Cabbage amuses him, even after months of the same show. He still laughs at all the corny jokes.

"Rough night?"

Blair spent her evening on the couch with her brother, drinking most of a bottle of wine and watching an old season of *The Real World*.

"I guess."

Nurse Vicki signals to Blair, agitated.

Emilio places a hand on her shoulder. "You're up."

It's Blair's job to take the freshly born doll into the doctor's room, a small pink room, with big glass windows where the kids and parents can watch a staff member perform a series of fake medical measures. She takes the doll's vitals. Weight, height, blood pressure—periodically lifting the doll up to wave to the ogling crowd. She emerges with a birth certificate and a carrying case for the birthday girl. Marley has chosen the name Kylie Peaches. Once Kylie Peaches is handed over, Marley squeezes her with all her six-year-old might.

"My baby."

⧗

Vicki arrives at Babyland before anyone else, flicking on the overhead lights until fluorescence hums above. Her routine, honed over the years, is a sacred ritual. She starts in the school room, methodically adjusting each doll at its tiny desk. Yarn-haired heads turn towards the oversized cloth teacher propped up at the front.

The nursery comes next. She places chubby-cheeked babies into pastel-lined cribs, tucking blankets around them with practiced efficiency. She dusts shelves lined with tiny shoes and bottles.

Sometimes, in these quiet moments, Vicki will take a doll and cradle it in the corner rocking chair. She sways back and forth, the weight in her arms a comforting illusion. *There, there.*

Vicki got married in 1979 and a decade later had given up on ever having children of her own. She tried and tried but her body never allowed it, and then her husband got sick, and priorities changed.

For years, Vicki kept the church nursery on Sundays. Muffled hymns drifted in as she watched babies grow, join their parents, get baptized, and return to the nursery with families of their own. There were always new babies to care for.

At 8:30 Vicki walks out to the main entrance and sees Emilio arriving, wiping his eyes. He never spoke much to Vicki, but always showed up right on time and greeted the guests with a level of enthusiasm she appreciated.

"Morning," she says and picks up a stray rubber band next to the sign-in sheet.

Birthday party days are Vicki's favorite. The facility feels so lively when a party is taking place; noisy and hopeful.

She spends a few minutes sweeping the floor of the party room and putting some pink and yellow cardboard party hats on the Cabbage Patch dolls. Setting their bobbing heads upright, she whispers to herself, "Perfect."

⏳

Emilio sits in his car, staring at his phone. There's a text from the football player:

Hey. Miss you. Can we talk?

Emilio's thumb hovers over the message. He types out several responses, deleting each one.

Finally, he pockets the phone without replying and heads inside. As he walks through the parking lot, he passes the giant Cabbage Patch Kid statues. He pauses, looking at their frozen, cheerful expressions.

"Morning," Nurse Vicki says as he enters, finishing her preparations for the day.

"Morning," Emilio responds, forcing a smile. He moves behind the front desk to put on his name tag. He hopes he doesn't look like he's spent the morning crying.

He boots up the computer, arranges the sign-in sheets, and prepares for another day of manufactured cheer and make-believe births. As the first customers of the day approach, Emilio takes a final steadying breath. Show time.

"Helloooo! Welcome to Babyland General Hospital." Emilio is relieved. "If I could have you sign in on this sheet before you head back," His tone is convincing. "That would be lovely." He pushes the sign-in sheet toward the blond family in matching red seersucker. The kid in the mom's arms is trying to jump out, reaching out toward Emilio.

"First time here?" He asks, waving gently at the reaching toddler.

"First time," The mom answers, somewhat exasperated. She switches the toddler to her other hip. The older boy, standing next to her leg, looks up at Emilio.

"We're going to a football game."

"Yes," The mom clarifies, "Heading down to Athens this afternoon."

Emilio raises his eyebrows, "And you get to stop in here first? What a lucky day."

The boy nods, eyeing his oblivious sister. "Dolls are for girls. For babies." As if this place made sense at any age.

Emilio bends down, eye level with the boy, and hands him a sticker with a Cabbage Patch head on it. He catches a glimpse of Blair, hurrying through the front door, her scrubs wrinkled. He smiles. "Dolls are for everyone."

⧗

After Marley and her friends have had their share of white frosting cake and apple juice, Emilio finds Blair in the break room eating a packet of toasted cheese crackers and scrolling on her phone. She barely looks up.

"Will you tell me something good?" Blair says, folding a leg up into the plastic chair that she's perched in and placing her phone on the table, screen down. "Something juicy?"

Emilio cracks a Coke, leaning against stark cabinets. The hostile lighting makes him self-conscious. Are his eyes still puffy? "Nothing to report," he shrugs.

Emilio had spent the summer divulging every thrilling detail of his love affair with the high school's star running back. How they exchanged a few flirty texts and then started meeting up in the drama club room during lunch. Their first kiss in the front seat of the athlete's truck. Everything, happening in secret. Exciting and devastating.

Emilio and Blair would pour over text messages searching for hidden meanings.

"He's actually so sweet," she said one afternoon in the lobby, holding Emilio's phone. It was open to a small list that the football player had sent to Emilio. All the reasons he liked him. *Your t-shirts.*

Blair's face falls. "Did something happen?"

Emilio looks down into his can of Coke. "I—"

"Alright, break's over." Nurse Vicki's head appears at the doorway and then disappears just as swiftly.

Blair stands up and reaches into a cabinet for a spray bottle of disinfectant and a dish rag. "She's not happy with me."

Emilio takes another sip of Coke before placing it back in the fridge. They walk out together, Emilio making his way to the loudspeaker at the front to announce yet another birth and Blair returning to the Birthday Party room to help Nurse Vicki undo the damage Marley and her friend's caused.

She's not surprised to find that Nurse Vicki has already done most of the clean up.

"Sorry I was late this morning," Blair says quietly, surprising herself with the level of sincerity in her tone. She knows this place is important to Nurse Vicki. More important than it is to her, Emilio, or most of the other staff members. When she first started, rumors were circulating that Nurse Vicki would take dolls home at night. She'd heard that there was a baby nursery next to Nurse Vicki's bedroom and that she would treat the dolls like real children, changing them into pajamas and waking up in the night to rock them. Someone even said they saw a car seat in her Camry.

At first, Blair was unsettled by the rumors, but as she got to know Nurse Vicki, it began to make more sense. She was lonely and while Blair couldn't understand the instinct to mother, she did understand loneliness.

"Just don't let it happen again," Nurse Vicki says.

Blair nods and begins to make her way out the door, eager to take her stethoscope off her neck and go on lunch break, but Nurse Vicki stops her.

"You know," Nurse Vicki says, tracing her finger along the colorful mural on the wall. "This place has been around for over forty years." Her eyes follow her finger. "250,000 people come through the doors each year."

Blair knows this spiel from orientation, but doesn't stop her.

"I was there when it first opened, back when it was still downtown." She looks at Blair who nods. "I had just gotten engaged." Her usual stern expression has transformed into something soft, making her look years younger.

"We went to the ribbon cutting and he bought me my first Cabbage Patch doll. Xavier signed it himself."

All the Cabbage Patch dolls had founder, Xavier Robert's signature on their ass, something that thoroughly disturbed Emilio and Blair. They would joke about getting it tattooed someday, once they had left the hospital and had new jobs. "You could get my signature and I could get yours," Emilio would say, smacking his own ass.

"We loved that doll so much, Blair." Nurse Vicki continues. "It's one of the few things I have left from him." Blair shifts her weight, unsure how to respond.

Nurse Vicki's eyes meet Blair's, and she appears to return to reality. "This is a special place, whether you think so or not." She doesn't blink. "So, please, just be on time."

⧗

Blair slumps onto the sun-warmed bench outside Babyland General, unwrapping her sandwich; a measly two slices of turkey she had thrown between some bread. She scrolls through Instagram with her spare hand, pausing on a photo of her former lab partner, now beaming in front of ivy-covered brick buildings.

She drops her phone into her lap just as Emilio plops down beside her.

"What is that?" he asks, eyeing her poor excuse of a lunch. "Looks awful."

She glares up at him. "Rough morning, remember?"

"I can pick you up something." Emilio sits down.

Blair shakes her head, accepting her shitty sandwich. They sit in silence, watching minivans and SUVs circle the parking lot. Blair's eyes follow a young couple entering the storefront, baby on hip. Her voice drops. "God, last year I thought I might have one of those."

Emilio looks at her, confused. "What, a sandwich?"

She glares at him, then nods towards the retreating family.

"Oh. Shit, Blair. I had no idea."

"Yeah, well." She crumples her sandwich wrapper. "Crisis averted, I guess."

Emilio considers placing his hand on Blair's shoulder for comfort, but stops himself.

"What's going on with you?" Blair finally asks. "I thought you and football guy were endgame."

Emilio lets out a laugh. "Yeah, I don't know. Turns out being someone's little secret isn't as romantic as the movies make it seem."

"He wouldn't–"

"He wouldn't even say hi to me in the light of day." Emilio shakes his head. "I get it, I do. But I couldn't do it anymore. I want... I don't know, a real life? Whatever that means."

A family walks by, leaving with their young daughter clutching a freshly adopted Cabbage Patch Kid to her chest. The parents kneel down to snap pictures as the girl beams.

Blair and Emilio exchange a look.

"Real life."

"Yeah," Emilio smiles, getting up and heading to his car. "Whatever that means."

⧗

Emilio returns from his lunch break with a greasy paper Bojangles bag filled with exceptionally seasoned fries.

"For the hangover," he says, sliding the bag towards Blair, across the break room table.

"Oh my god, lifesaver," She immediately takes a handful, hoping the starch and salt will finally do the trick.

Emilio glances at his phone, winces at a wall of blue text, and pockets it quickly. "Back to it," he sighs, heading towards Mother Cabbage for the afternoon birth.

The fluorescent lights flicker as Emilio's finger hovers over the intercom button. He takes a deep breath, closes his eyes for a moment, then presses down.

"Dilation is at 8 leaves!" His voice echoes through the store. "All staff to Mother Cabbage for an imminent birth!"

Emilio weaves through the gathering crowd, nodding at the excited faces of children tugging on their parents' sleeves and taking his place by Mother Cabbage.

"Ladies and gentlemen," he begins, his voice quieter than usual. A few heads in the back crane to hear him. Emilio clears his throat and tries again, this time projecting to the back of the crowd. "Ladies and gentlemen, boys and girls!"

A child in the front row giggles, and something shifts in Emilio. His posture straightens, his gestures become more expansive. "Mother Cabbage is ready to bring another beautiful Cabbage Patch Kid into the world!"

He reaches for the oversized syringe of Imagicillin, twirling it in his hands like a baton. "First, we need to make sure Mother Cabbage is comfortable. Who wants to help me give her some Imagicillin?"

A forest of small hands shoots up. Emilio picks a shy-looking boy near the back. As the child presses the plunger, Emilio lets out an exaggerated sigh of relief. "Ahhh, much better! Can you feel the magic in the air?"

The crowd leans in, captivated. Emilio's voice rises and falls dramatically as he narrates the birth. He mimics the contractions of Mother Cabbage, his face contorting in exaggerated pain that has the children both concerned and delighted.

"It's time to push!" Emilio calls out. "Everyone, on the count of three, yell 'PUSH' as loud as you can! One... two... three!"

The room erupts in a chorus of "PUSH!" Emilio reaches into Mother Cabbage's roots, his movements deliberate and theatrical. With a flourish, he pulls out a doll, holding it high above his head.

"It's a girl!" he announces as the crowd cheers.

Emilio cradles the doll, gently wiping its forehead, and then his own with a cloth.

As he hands the doll to Blair for vitals, she gives him a thumbs up, mouthing "Wow." It was his best performance yet.

⧗

The last birth ends and Blair finds herself straightening shelves near the adoption center. Her mind is still on the lunchtime conversation with Emilio. She pushes away worries that she shared too much.

A flash of red catches her eye. A little girl with curly auburn hair, no more than five or six, wanders away from her distracted parents. The child reaches for a doll on a high shelf, her small fingers grasping at air.

Blair watches, waiting to see if the parents will notice. They don't. With a sigh, she approaches.

"Need some help?"

The girl nods shyly, pointing to a 1996 Olympic-themed doll. Blair reaches for it, but as she does, the girl bumps into the shelf. The doll tumbles down, along with several others.

"Oh shi—shoot," Blair mutters, dropping to her knees to gather the fallen dolls. The little girl's eyes well up.

"Hey, accidents happen. Want to help me pick them up?"

The girl nods, sniffling, and begins carefully placing dolls back on the shelf. Blair watches her small hands move with surprising care.

Blair picks up the Olympic doll the girl had been reaching for. She holds it out in front of her and really looks at it for the first time. Its big eyes stare back, its rounded nose slightly askew. Red yarn sprouts from its soft head in unruly curls.

Hideous, Blair thinks. But as she looks from the doll to the little girl, she sees something she hadn't before.

"You know," Blair says, "she kind of looks like you."

The girl's eyes widen, a mix of surprise and delight. "Really?"

Blair nods. "Yeah, look at those curls. And those freckles? Definitely twins."

The girl giggles, reaching for the doll. Blair hands it over, watching as small arms wrap around it in a fierce hug.

"I love her," the girl lisps.

⧗

As the last visitors file out, Nurse Vicki begins her nightly routine. She moves through the nursery, straightening tiny bonnets and adjusting blankets with care.

In the back room, she pauses at a locked cabinet. With a quick glance to ensure she's alone, she opens it, revealing a worn Cabbage Patch doll. The signature is faded but still legible: Xavier Roberts.

Vicki cradles the doll, her eyes misty. "Hello, Charlie," she whispers, running a hand over its yarn hair. "Did you have a good day?"

She walks to the rocking chair in the corner, sitting down with Charlie. As she rocks, she speaks softly.

"Red hair, just like Daddy's." She holds him to her chest, feeling his heartbeat against hers. "Just perfect."

THE COMPUTER ROOM

In real life, I'm eight-and-a-half years old, but on babynames.com/messageboards I'm closer to thirty-one.

It's summer and I spend my days at my best friend and next-door neighbor's house, upstairs in her computer room, surrounded by our sleeping bags. Her name is Liz.

I love the computer room at Liz's because I love the internet and playing games like *The Sims*. My family doesn't have a computer yet. Some nights, we play *The Sims* until after midnight, because it's summer and we can do that. There's nothing to wake up early for.

Liz likes to kill her Sims with indoor fireworks, but I like when mine fall in love and make a baby.

We keep the TV on TLC all day because we've decided we're too old for Disney Channel but nothing else is interesting yet. Liz watches *Trading Spaces*, where two neighbors swap houses and redecorate a room in each other's homes. She even tried to sign us up on tlc.com but they never wrote us back.

My favorite show is *A Baby Story* because I like the babies on *The Sims* so much. In every episode of *A Baby Story*, a couple is pregnant, gives birth, and then names the baby. I know all about giving birth from watching this show. I know about a C-section and an epidural. I know about breastfeeding. My mom didn't tell me about any of it, but it was easy to figure out, from the show.

When a Sim gives birth, the computer screen zooms in on her, even if you are far away, doing something else with another Sim. She waves her hand around and makes a concerned expression. She kind of spins into a cloud of pixels and suddenly is holding a baby. You have to buy the baby a crib and stuff because if the Sim doesn't have one, it'll put the baby on the floor. And if you do that enough times, someone will come and take the baby away, and then your Sim becomes depressed—which is really hard to come back from, without using a cheat code.

Liz uses cheat codes all the time, but I try to play *The Sims* honestly.

After Liz shows me tlc.com, from when we tried to sign up for *Trading Spaces*, I go look at *A Baby Story*'s page. You can click on all the couples and see a photo of their baby now. Most of the babies are just a little bit older. Sitting up and stuff like that. I see one from an episode I just watched. The baby is named Mackenzie, which I think is just beautiful. I've never heard of anyone with such a pretty name.

I close out of tlc.com, returning to the homepage and type into the search bar, "baby names," using just my index fingers. I learn that the name Mackenzie means "son of Kenneth." Ew, who is Kenneth?

My mom works all day in the summer which is why I spend so much time at Liz's house. Liz has an older brother who is home for summer, too, but who is old enough to watch us. He doesn't though, he just plays *Nintendo* in his room.

While Liz makes frozen tater tots in the oven for our lunch, I look up more baby names.

My own name means "smart" which I like. Liz's means "God's promise" which makes me think about rainbows. I learned in Sunday school that those have the same meaning. God's promise.

My Sim is pregnant again because I made her Woo-Hoo in the heart-shaped hot tub nine times in a row until her sleep bar was so low, she had to take a nap and missed her job at the newspaper.

"What are you gonna name it?" Liz asks me, hopping around on the couch behind the computer, holding a soda. A big plate of tater tots covered in ketchup sits on the carpet in front of her.

This question gives me a feeling of responsibility, now that I'm becoming somewhat of a name expert. I make an account on babynames.com. Momof4expecting. I act like I'm a Sim or maybe like I'm on TLC's *A Baby Story*. Like I have a real big belly of my own.

Hello namers, I am a mom of 4 and I am pregnate again. I do not know if it's a boy or a girl but we hope girl. The others are named Allie, Kayla, Lance (after Lance bass) and Carly. What should I name the new baby?

I type all that out and read it back over to make sure I sound like a real adult woman who is responsible enough to have four children, a loving husband, and a computer of her own. I hit send while Liz jumps around behind me, licking ketchup off her fingers.

Liz and I once pretended to be her brother in his AOL messages. We sent the same message to his whole buddy list, just saying Wazzup. Some people answered and we giggled about it but she got too nervous to keep it up.

"It's dishonest." Liz said, which I thought was funny given how many cheat codes she uses.

I print off lists of names in order of their popularity, which is something I find on babynames.com and is something that fascinates me.

I think it's fun to memorize them and it makes me feel "smart" like my own name implies. The Number 1 name in 1992, the year I was born, was Ashley. I know six of them. I'm Number 211 which is pretty unique.

"Names are boring," Liz says, picking up the throw pillows on the couch and tossing them to the side. "Can we play *Trading Spaces* again?"

We play *Trading Spaces* by having one of us cover our eyes while the other rearranges the computer room. Liz likes to print photos of the Backstreet Boys straight from Yahoo images and tape them up on the walls.

"Surprise!" she says when I open my eyes, revealing a new photo of Nick Carter and a different arrangement of pillows. This time they were stacked one on top of the other in the middle of the couch.

"It's beautiful!" I say, doing my best to act so surprised. "I love it in here."

My Sim gets more and more pregnant, even though I am trying hard not to fast forward the time—even when they're all sleeping.

I log back into babynames.com to see what all the other moms think of my big naming dilemma.

> AldermanFamily07: Hailey for a girl and Brice for a boy.

> JThomas80: 5 kids wow! What are their middle names? Taylor seems like a good fit, boy or girl.

I look up the meaning of Taylor which is "tailor" and feel disappointed.

Hailey does seem like a good choice but is also the name of a girl who was in my class last year who I didn't like very much. She was always the first one to get to the swings at recess and would sit in the middle swing, holding onto the ropes of the two on either side, saving them for her best friends. This never seemed very fair to me and also meant that I never got to go on the swings.

I couldn't name my Sim baby after a person like that.

> Momoftwinz says I can't believe you named your baby after Lance Bass.

I tell Liz that I didn't get very many good suggestions on the website, and she says, "Move over." I roll away from the keyboard and she takes my place, standing up in front of it with a wild look in her eyes.

She clicks NEW POST from my account and types:

> Help urgent, in labor right now!!! Need a name right now!!!!! Nothing dumb

I gasp and then giggle as she hits send.

"Get off the internet, I need to call Cam!" Liz's brother yells from down the hall.

"Who's Cam?" I ask as I disconnect, clearing the phone lines.

Liz rolls her eyes. "My brother's dumb friend." She powers down the computer. "They started a dumb band together."

"Liz!" He yells again.

"We're offline!!!" She yells back, even louder. I wince.

Liz falls to the floor, dramatically, spreading her arms out like a snow angel. "I'm bored."

Between TLC episodes, home improvements to the computer room, and lengthy sessions of *The Sims*, Liz and I don't usually have a lot of time for much else.

"Maybe I should go home," I suggest, reluctantly. My mom has been out with her boyfriend the past three nights, so I haven't slept in my own bed in days.

Liz sits up. "No!" She grabs my wrist. "We need to get back online and see if anyone has replied. We're in labor."

I think about my Sim family, frozen somewhere in time. It really wasn't urgent at all. The baby wasn't growing without the computer on, plus we'd saved the game. Everything would be just as it was whenever Liz's brother was off the phone and we could get back on.

Liz throws me my shoes and slips on her own jelly sandals. "Let's walk to the library."

The library is just a couple of blocks from where Liz and I live. I used to go a lot as a younger kid, back when my mom didn't work so much and didn't have a boyfriend. She would take me and Liz to story time and let us each check out a book.

When the library got their computers, my mom would take me with her to print out her resumés and look at her match.com profile. I loved to sit in her lap while she scrolled and scrolled.

Liz and I walk in to the library. It's dimly lit and smells old, but familiar.

"We need a computer," Liz says confidently to the lady at the front desk with big gold glasses and a curly, too-short, haircut.

"I'm sorry girls but the computers are only for twelve and up." She tilts her chin down and looks at us over the top of her glasses. "Unless you have an adult with you."

Liz frowns. "You're an adult, aren't you?"

I wish the library was like the babynames.com website, where I could be thirty-one if I needed to be.

"I'm sorry," the woman says, turning around to put some little white slips in some books.

"Come back with a parent."

Liz and I exchange disappointed glances.

"Do you have any books on baby names?" I ask, knowing that the books are for everyone, even if you're only eight.

The librarian looks confused but starts typing into her monitor.

"Um, yes, I believe so." Clack, clack, clack. "Aisle Seven in resources."

I check out two books and sit with Liz on the sidewalk, flipping through them.

"I want my Sim to have a name that means beautiful," I say, turning the page. The book is old and faded, resting awkwardly on my knees. "Or loved."

Sweat starts to bead around Liz's forehead. She closes the book for me and says, "I'm hungry." We fish around in our pockets for some change and decide to get Slurpees on the way home. The guy at the gas station on the corner is familiar with us and will take whatever change we have. This is a benefit of being eight years old.

We slam the screen door to Liz's house and kick off our shoes, tired from the walk and the summer heat but beginning to feel the rush of sugar from the drinks.

Liz's brother emerges from his room in basketball shorts and no shirt. He always looks like he just woke up.

"Your mom called," he says to me, running his hand through his mess of hair. "She wants you to stay here again tonight," I try and hide my disappointment.

"We can play *The Sims*!" Liz offers, even though I know she's getting tired of it. She reaches for the library book in my hand. "Let's pick out the name. For the baby."

Liz's brother mutters something about us being "so weird" and retreats to his room. I've never seen the inside of his bedroom, but I imagine that it's dark and full of posters of the bands he likes. I'd guess that there are shirts in there, even though I have never seen them.

My Sim is going to give birth at any moment and the moms on the babynames.com message boards still haven't come up with anything good.

Liz and I sift through our replies, which are mostly just people expressing concern and wondering how we are able to use the internet while in labor.

The last reply is from DancerMom27 who says:

    I wonder if I'm too late. Have you considered Rose?
    Please let us know what you decide <3

Rose.

I say it out loud. "Rose."

It's so simple. I know the meaning without even having to look it up. Allie, Kayla, Lance Jr., Carly, and *Rose*.

My Sim lifts her hand in the air, before grabbing at her pixelated belly.

"It's happening…" I whisper. Liz takes a sip of her Slurpee, sucking up mostly air and the last dribbles of cherry syrup. She runs over to the computer screen. A blue box pops up, pausing the game. Congrats! It's a girl. I'm prompted to type in the name, so I carefully press the R, followed by the O. The S. The E. Baby Rose. I make a small vow in my mind to love and care for Rose, as best as I can. When my Sim makes enough money at her newspaper job, maybe Rose could even have her own room, away from all these siblings. I begin to understand why Liz uses cheat codes to get more money. I want to give Rose everything.

"She's beautiful," I say to Liz, even though all Sim babies look the same until they eventually morph into toddlers. My Sim is ecstatic. Her happiness levels are sky-high, even though she hasn't showered in a while and needs to eat lunch. She rocks Baby Rose in her arms as plus signs fly out from the top of her head.

I make sure to hit save just in case.

"Happy Birthday, Rose!" Liz says, springing up onto the couch with her empty Slurpee cup. She does one jump into the air and lands seated, criss-cross style. "Do you want to watch a movie?"

I nod and head to the bathroom, full of Slurpee.

When I return to the computer room, flicking sink water off my hands, Liz is printing out pictures of roses to hang up on the wall.

COUSINS

lla opens her eyes and rolls over. Pain. She keeps forgetting. She had dreamt she was running. Dancing. Leaping through the air. The black swan, doing thirty-two fouettés turns in a forest of kudzu and tall oak trees.

It takes her a good two minutes to sit up. She presses the side button of her Blackberry and sees 9:05 a.m. It's a Monday morning in May, and her friends are all starting their last month of freshman year.

In a different timeline, she would be in Latin 1, cheating off Paige on a vocabulary test. And probably, Audrey would be cheating off her. She thinks briefly about the broken chain and hopes Audrey has the good sense to move up a seat in her absence.

She groans louder than intended.

"Ella?" A voice from downstairs. "Ella, are you awake?"

Ella wiggles her toes experimentally. She's been paranoid, since her surgery, that one of these days she'll wake up paralyzed, even though the risk of that is virtually over.

"Yeah—" she tries to yell, but her voice croaks. She clears her throat. Her pain medicine makes her dehydrated.

"Yeah, I'm awake." She stands and steadies herself. The staircase scares her mother, so she tries to be cautious. "I'm coming down."

Libby is standing at the bottom of the stairs holding the remote and a large cup of ice filled with Diet Mountain Dew. She's wearing an oversized sorority t-shirt and looks at Ella with a weird mix of empathy and fear. Like she doesn't want to watch her struggle but knows that she's supposed to.

"You're here early," Ella says, gripping the railing and placing both feet onto each step carefully as she descends.

"Your mom told me nine." Libby reaches out a hand, but Ella rejects it. "She just left."

"I'm fine."

"I'm supposed to give you your medicine."

Ella walks to the cabinet in small, baby shuffles. "I've got it."

Libby raises her eyebrows in surrender and sits back down on the couch. She's watching MTV, which is playing a rerun of a recent episode of *Laguna Beach*. She turns the volume back up.

On the screen, beautiful California teenagers with perfect hair are going to Cabo for spring break. Even from the kitchen, it sounds silly to Ella. Not at all like the brief seven months of high school she's already experienced. It was just her own spring break, and she spent it in a hospital in Atlanta, having her spine restructured.

"Do you watch this show?" Libby asks.

Ella swallows her pills in one big gulp and slowly makes her way to the couch next to Libby. She scoots over so Ella can lie down, keeping her back straight and flat.

"Not really, it's kind of…" Ella hesitates. "Dumb."

"Yeah."

"You like it?"

Libby doesn't take her eyes away from the television. "It's fine. It was always on at the sorority house."

"Right."

On the screen, Steven has put on a fake bear suit to scare his two crushes. Ella finds it amusing but stifles her laughter. It's almost ten o'clock. She'd be in second period, P.E., which is something she can't imagine ever doing again. It doesn't feel like a huge loss.

She never liked to run or play sports. She liked to dance, but even that feels like something from the past she may never get back. Ballet was something she was good at, but that she associated with a delicate femininity she never quite possessed. Nearly everyone in her family was good at ballet, which stubbornly made her want to resist it.

As soon as Ella reached middle school, she started to hang out with kids who skated or played in bands. Kids who wrote poetry on Xanga and stuck safety pins through their tongues in the cafeteria.

It was a far cry from the world of her aunt—Libby's mother—a professional dancer who owned a studio in their hometown. It was there, doing forward rolls on the solid black flooring in sixth grade, that Ella first learned of the curvature in her spine. Tiny, dotted bruises formed along her back in the S shape she'd come to know intimately on X-ray screens. Her aunt changed the choreography so she wouldn't have to do them anymore, and she started seeing doctors regularly.

"I'm sorry this is your job," Ella says to her cousin as the *Laguna Beach* credits begin to roll. Hilary Duff wails through the speakers. She looks down at her body, frail and foreign to her. "That I'm your job."

"Oh, stop feeling sorry, Ella," Libby flips the channel to the news. Something about war, something about Iraq. "Let's just admit this is probably not the summer either of us had in mind and try to make the best of it."

⧗

Audrey made Ella a mixed CD with "Get well soon" written in Sharpie on the front and little flowers drawn around the perimeter. She placed it on Ella's doorstep before she even got home from the hospital. When Ella discovered it, she held it in her hand, like something precious and delicate, tracing her fingers over the text lightly, not leaving a mark.

Ella played it in her stereo every morning while getting ready and staring at her spine, wrapped in blood-dotted gauze, in the mirror. Snow Patrol and Sufjan Stevens—stuff her other friends weren't listening to.

Audrey and Ella had first bonded over her Sigur Rós MySpace song, exchanging messages back and forth on AIM and sharing links to music videos. Glósóli was their favorite. The way the Icelandic kids just ran right off the cliff and flew. Magic.

Before the surgery, Audrey took Ella to her first punk show, where kids from the county schools went to get drunk and throw themselves around. Ella instinctively knew to lie, saying she was at Paige's. Paige, whose spine probably grew straight out of sheer obedience.

Audrey had met most of the people there on MySpace. Jeremy with his mohawk, Josh in jeans that reminded Ella of her ballet tights. Everyone smoked cigarettes, which seemed to be the main point of being there, even more than listening to the band.

Audrey would get right up front and throw her body around to the music in a way Ella admired. Something so different from the way she'd been trained to move–precise and poised.

Audrey would stumble back from the pit, foam-splattered and limping. "Someone broke my toe," she'd laugh into Ella's ear, arm slung over her shoulder. The closeness made Ella dizzy.

Then there was the kiss. One night in the park, fueled by vodka mixed with Crystal Light in a water bottle. Audrey's AIM message: come to the park!! don't be a loser, saved forever in a Word doc on Ella's computer.

"You've never kissed anyone?" Audrey had asked, incredulous. She leaned in, streetlight making her skin glow. "Kiss me, then," she whispered, and suddenly their lips met. Messy, urgent. Tasting of aspartame and cheap liquor. When Audrey pulled away, she grinned like she'd just invented something. "See? Easy." Jeremy, climbing a nearby fence, saw nothing.

⧗

The neon cactus of Los Poblanos flickers as Libby pulls into the parking lot. She spots Peyton's truck and Tara's beat-up Civic, already there.

Inside, the smell of stale beer and enchiladas hit her. Tara waves from their usual booth, Blockbuster name tag still pinned to her shirt.

Libby slides in next to her. Peyton is already halfway through a basket of chips, salsa smeared on the corner of his mouth.

"You missed happy hour," he says, mouth full.

Libby reaches for a chip and lies, "Traffic. Fridays."

The waiter appears, notepad in hand. "The usual?"

Before Libby can respond, Tara jumps in. "Yes please, and can we get some extra limes?" She couldn't remember all that much about Tara from school, even though they'd basically grown up together. They had physics together junior year, or maybe it was health class?

As the waiter leaves, Libby leans back, taking in the familiar scene. A group of middle-aged women celebrating a birthday in the corner. The high school history teacher they often avoid, eating fajitas silently across from his wife. The same mariachi cover of "Sweet Home Alabama" playing for the third time; a cruel reminder of the football games and rowdy college bars she'd left behind.

"So," Peyton says, wiping his mouth with the back of his hand. "What's new with the kid?"

Libby shrugs. "Ella's fine. We watch a lot of MTV."

"Paid to watch TV," Tara's tone is sarcastic but she seems genuinely envious. "The dream."

Libby feels Peyton's hand find the small of her back and she resists the urge to arch away. "Something like that."

Ella's eyes drift to the mixed CD propped against her computer monitor, Audrey's familiar handwriting still visible on the cover. She hasn't played it in a while, the case collecting a thin film of dust. The quiet of the computer room is broken by the familiar sounds of AIM. The door slams as someone signs on. xXpunkprincessXx. Before she can decide whether to message her or not, a window pops up.

    xXpunkprincessXx: hey stranger

    balletrebel15: hey

    xXpunkprincessXx: how r u feeling??

    balletrebel15: ok i guess. bored.

    xXpunkprincessXx: that sucks :(

    balletrebel15: yeah

    xXpunkprincessXx:: jeremy says hi btw

    balletrebel15: cool

    xXpunkprincessXx: we miss u at shows :(

    balletrebel15: yeah

Ella's fingers hover over the keyboard. The cursor blinks, a steady rhythm against the sound of Libby munching on chips from the couch.

She glances at the window, where the late afternoon sun casts long shadows across her neighbor's lawn. Libby would be leaving soon.

    xXpunkprincessXx: well, ttyl i guess

Ella closes the chat window, exhaling slowly. A chip arcs through the air, landing with a soft thud against Ella's head.

"Hey," she protests, swiveling in her chair. A twinge shoots through her back.

Libby glances at her watch. "Get off that thing. We've got time for one more episode before I have to go."

Ella eases onto the couch as the *Laguna Beach* prom episode flickers to life. On screen, guys vie for dates with increasingly elaborate gestures, but Ella's attention drifts. She pictures Audrey at the punk shows returning, sweaty, bright and giggling, to Jeremy. Kissing him late at night on the park bench.

⧖

After four days of nothing but *Laguna Beach* reruns on the couch, Libby asks Ella if she's healed enough to go lay by a pool.

"I figure it's just like the couch." She shrugs. "I could bring a pillow?"

Ella agrees and puts on the one strappy black bikini that her mom hates, taking a moment to admire how the bow in the back highlights her blood-crusted stitches.

They listen to Nelly's song with Tim McGraw in the car and blast the AC. It's not yet summer, but the Georgia humidity has already taken over. They go to the neighborhood pool several blocks over, on Peyton's street. Ella's doctor told her to take a daily walk as she healed. She counts the journey from Libby's car to the pool chair as her exercise, careful with each step.

Peyton is already there, lying on a folding chair. He has a new Razr phone that he keeps flipping open and snapping shut—punctuation to his low, disgruntled murmur. Ella watches Libby watch him, puzzling over the allure.

"He was my boyfriend in tenth grade," Libby had explained on the way over. Ella has a faint memory of this, did he come to Thanksgiving dinner one year or is she getting him confused with someone else? He still looks at her like she's seven.

"Is he your boyfriend again?" Ella tried to hide her judgment but her tone betrayed her.

"He's really not so bad."

Peyton starts doing flips in the pool, emerging to shake out his hair like an overgrown puppy.

Ella shifts uncomfortably in her cheap plastic pool chair, pointing her toes and feeling a familiar stretch. "Do you miss ballet?" She asks.

The question hangs for a moment as Libby's eyes follow Peyton before turning back to Ella. She takes a long sip from her Diet Mountain Dew.

"Sometimes," Libby finally admits. "But not in the way you'd think."

Ella waits. She knows bits and pieces of Libby's dance history—a patchwork of overheard conversations and family lore. Libby had been great, everyone said so. But there was always an undercurrent, a "but" that followed the praise.

"I miss the feeling right before a performance," Libby continues. "When anything seems possible, you know? Before reality sets in."

Ella nods, thinking not of ballet but of punk shows and Audrey.

"But the rest of it?" Libby shakes her head. "The criticism, the pressure, all the expectations. I don't miss any of that."

"Is that why you quit? The pressure?"

Libby's face tightens. "I told you, I wasn't that good."

"Mom says you could've gone pro."

"Oh, yeah?" Libby takes another sip from her Diet Mountain Dew cup, shaking around the ice, looking for the last of it. "My mom says the same about you."

⧗

It's Saturday, so Ella is with her mom, and Peyton is off playing golf. Libby wakes up bored and considers just going over to Ella's anyway. Maybe they could start a new show—*The OC* is supposed to be good. Of course, she wouldn't be getting paid, but it sounds more fun than anything else she can come up with. She feels embarrassed that on a bright, sunny day with no plans, she still wants to hang out with her fourteen-year-old cousin. If she was still in Alabama, she might visit the pool at the apartment complex with the tiki bar or sit at her favorite coffee shop downtown, people-watching.

Instead, Libby decides to visit Tara at Blockbuster. The store is nearly empty at eleven a.m., and the bright overhead lights reflect off every glossy DVD cover. It smells like carpet and old candy. Tara is behind the counter in a royal blue vest and greets her without looking up as if she's any old customer, coming in with a purpose.

"Hey Tara," She leans against the counter.

"Oh, hey." Tara has thick eyeliner drawn on her lower lids, and her hair is pulled into a messy side braid. "It's you."

Tara tells Libby about the man who waits outside until Blockbuster opens and immediately goes to the back for the porn. She's glad it was Libby walking through the fingerprint-stained double doors and not him.

"I'm supposed to set up a display for the *Shrek 2* release," Tara says, gesturing to a green headband with alien-like Shrek ears attached, lying ominously by the cash register. "I can't bring myself to do it yet."

"I saw the first one; it was pretty good."

"Kids love it."

There's an awkward pause where Tara realizes there's no real reason Libby is here, except maybe boredom.

"How's babysitting?"

Libby considers saying, *She's not really a baby*; she's got this whole life. But she shrugs instead.

"It's fine, she's with her mom today."

Tara places the Shrek ears on top of her head and pulls out her bangs so they hang down in front of the band, grazing her eyebrow.

"This is so awful."

"It's cute on you."

"Wanna help?" Tara begins pulling a cardboard cutout of a cartoon donkey from a large brown box.

Libby nods and moves around the counter. They start assembling the display, Tara struggling with the life-sized donkey while Libby arranges DVDs in a haphazard tower.

Tara grunts, wrestling with the creature's floppy paper ears. "My sister had to take a semester off last year, too."

Libby tenses slightly, focusing intently on her DVD arrangement. "Oh, yeah?"

"Sometimes things just don't go as planned, you know?" The donkey ears spring up, causing Tara to jump and then burst into a fit of giggles.

Libby places the final *Shrek 2* DVD on the tower and steps back to admire her work. "Hey, do y'all have *The OC*? We're probably gonna finish *Laguna Beach* soon and I haven't seen it yet."

The doorbell chimes as an older man in a worn leather jacket enters the store, avoiding eye contact. He shuffles towards the back, past their half-finished display.

"I still can't believe your whole job is to watch dumb shows with a fourteen-year-old," Tara says, though her job seems even more absurd, at this moment.

"Take her *Shrek 2*, too." Tara carefully removes the top DVD, bracing the rest for a potential tumble that never comes. "If no one rents these, we have to pay a fee."

⧖

For the most part, the days feel indistinguishable. But as late May comes, Ella's stamina increases. She agrees to go to the mall with Libby to look for a birthday present for Peyton. He's turning 23 at the end of the month, and Libby wants to get him a watch.

"He is a fan of the Auburn Tigers, even though *I* went to Alabama," she explains. "I don't know if I could bring myself to get him an Auburn watch, but I bet he'd really love it." The mall is mostly dead at one p.m. on a Thursday, except for the retired mall walkers and moms with young kids buying those cookie sandwiches with icing in the middle.

"Let's go to American Eagle and see what they have there," Libby suggests, turning a corner.

Ella recognizes a figure with long, swooping bangs and pale legs in the distance heading in her direction. Audrey, with Josh and his barely-there mustache, car keys hanging from his pocket. Behind them, Jeremy, with new green streaks painted into his mohawk and a few other nameless kids that she's seen at the punk shows. Audrey sees her too, face falling and rising just as dramatically as she skips hurriedly toward Ella and Libby. Ella braces herself for an incoming hug. "Be careful," someone whispers, and Audrey slows down. She touches Ella's shoulder gently.

"Are y'all skipping school?" Libby asks, confused, and then after an awkward silence, "I mean, no judgment." Ella watches Libby's eyes trace the whole crew up and down.

"We were just at Hot Topic," Audrey says, holding a tiny, branded plastic bag up to her face like it's evidence in a trial. She glances at Libby and, sensing her authority, exaggerates a cough, "But yeah, we're uh…sick today." She pulls out dangling skull earrings from the black plastic bag. "Look at these!"

Ella reaches out to touch the cheap metal. "Woah."

"Don't you like them?" She looks at both Libby and Ella.

"I love them," Ella holds them up, still in their cardboard, to her own ear. The best Libby can offer is a half-smile and diverted eye contact.

"Well," Audrey says, "see you on AIM, I guess." She gallops ahead to catch up with the others, who have begun walking toward the cookie place. Through the quiet of the mall, Ella catches Josh's voice, low and eager: "Hey, you think she's got any of those good painkillers?" Someone laughs, hitting him on the shoulder. Audrey doesn't seem to react.

"You hang out with people like that?" Libby asks in the car, driving home, the Auburn watch wrapped in a delicate bow, lying between them in the cup holder. Ella can't tell if Libby is genuinely curious or having some sort of pseudo-parental concern.

"No." She turns up the AC, feeling the sweat around her hairline instantly cool. "I only hang out with you."

⧗

Ella and Libby make it to the season finale of *Laguna Beach*—the graduation episode. Ella blinks away tears, embarrassed by her genuine investment in their tender goodbyes. Maybe she really believes in Lo and LC's friendship. She can tell they care about each other from the way they sing along to the same songs in the car or communicate their sarcasm with just a glance. Now they have to move away from each other to begin the rest of their lives, and the Vitamin C-tracked montage isn't helping.

"Most of 'em will come back, is the thing," Libby says, eyes still glued to the TV. "They're hopeful now, but they don't really know."

Libby has stayed at Ella's, watching TV, long past 4 p.m. She is no longer getting paid to be there. Her flip phone keeps buzzing on the table between them, but she's ignoring it. Ella thinks it must be Peyton. Maybe he's trying to invite her out to the Mexican restaurant or some party at his neighborhood pool. She pictures him snapping his phone, open and closed, between each call, Auburn Tigers watch on his wrist.

Ella's mom asks if Libby's staying for dinner, and it looks as if she's really contemplating it, but after finally opening her phone to all of the missed calls, she grabs her keys.

"I better just go, but thank you." She waves goodbye to Ella. "See you Monday."

In the car, Libby turns up the radio nearly as high as it will go. She drives down the main road thinking about how many times she must have done this exact drive now. 500? 1,000? She remembers her dad sitting shotgun beside her when she was Ella's age, saying, "You got this, look, you're doing it!" as her knuckles turned white.

She slows down as she passes Los Poblanos, eyeing Peyton's truck and Tara's civic out front, but she doesn't stop. She continues down the familiar roads, past her old high school, past the park where all the punk kids hang out, and then the Sonic, where you could sit on top of your car and drink a lemon slushie until midnight, if you wanted.

The sun starts to set as crunchy static interrupts a Rascal Flatts song, returning as something else entirely. She drives to the parking lot of her mom's dance studio.

It's closed, and all the lights are off — Friday classes always end early. The lot is empty, so she keeps her headlights on and gets out of her car, leaving the door open and the new country song playing. She's on stage, standing there with the lights pointing at her. She lifts her arm up and bends her leg, raising the other into an arabesque. She pulls her foot forward, landing in fourth position, turning, turning, turning. She follows her fingers, stretched long in front of her, with her eyes. Energy ripples through her body as she stretches it, leaping on the asphalt.

She doesn't wonder if her leg is as high as it used to be or if her foot is sickled in her sandals. Fouetté after fouetté, but she's not counting. It's dizzying, with nowhere to spot, as the headlights blur around her. She collapses as the song ends, and a radio voice comes in like a disembodied prophet, saying something about the weather. *"Real hot one tonight, folks."* Sweat has beaded onto her forehead, and she breathes heavily, touching her palms to the burning ground. *"Be careful out there."*

She folds her knees into her chest, noticing the way her patchy knee hairs shimmer in the headlights. She thinks to herself, *I was right*. She thinks, *I don't miss that*.

⧗

Ella sits in the harsh glow of her family's computer screen, scrolling.

Audrey has changed her MySpace song from their matching Sigur Rós song to something by Interpol. Her profile picture is now a heavily saturated photo of her and Jeremy. Their heads tilted towards each other, taken by Audrey's arm, too high above their heads. The angle makes their darkly-lined eyes look huge, and her bangs look longer than they really are.

She can see the new little skull earrings, one in each of their lobes. Touching, but just slightly.

Ella shuts off the computer and walks out the back door and down the neighborhood street. It's hot and sticky. Each house sits eerily quiet, dark, and identical to the one next to it. She contemplates running, wondering if her spine might surprise her with sudden cooperation. She could tombé, pas de bourrée, glissade, jeté, right down the center of the asphalt.

She texts Libby, "Pick me up?" and Libby almost immediately replies, "On my way".

When Libby pulls up Ella has taken a seat on the curb. Long walks still make her winded. Libby rolls the window down.

"You okay?"

Ella nods and pulls her knees into her chest before standing up to climb into the passenger seat.

"How's Peyton," Ella asks dryly.

"Don't know." Libby begins looping around the cul-de-sacs aimlessly. "Went for a drive instead. Does your mom know you're out?"

Ella shakes her head, no, so they drive silently over winding roads, only passing another car every few minutes. Ella stares out the window and tries not to think about Audrey or school or that dumb little earring. She doesn't think about what her feet would feel like hitting the concrete or if her back will ever bend enough to properly land a tour jeté again.

When they are far enough away from Ella's neighborhood, she eyes the steering wheel and asks, "Can I try?" Libby pulls over to swap seats.

She shows Ella exactly where to place her hands and feet, how much pressure to use, and when to look in each mirror.

"See, it's really not so hard."

Ella is careful around turns but speeds up when the road straightens out. They glance at each other and smile.

"Faster?" Libby asks, hand raised, rolling down the sunroof.

Ella's dark hair catches in the cool night air and dances sharply around Libby's blonde. She presses down on the gas.

30-DAY SONG CHALLENGE

Day 1: A song that reminds you of being nine years old and drinking honeysuckles in the backyard after piano class while your mom pays the teacher.

Day 2: A song that you listened to while driving on the interstate for the first time, even though you weren't allowed, and you got off one exit from where you got on because you were nervous.

Day 3: A cover song that you never knew was a cover until someone at a party, where you were already feeling self-conscious anyway, made you feel really stupid about it and now it's the only thing you can remember when you think back on that party.

Day 4: A song your coworker would always play, and it used to annoy you but now you kind of love it and want to tell them, but you probably won't.

Day 5: A song that you only ever listened to thirty seconds of because it was on a "hit clip" that you got inside of a Happy Meal.

Day 6: A song by someone you personally know that comes on shuffle—every time, like a cruel joke—when you are just trying to make out and not think about your friends.

Day 7: A song that always makes you think "I should do this at karaoke" but then you forget when you are actually at karaoke, and you just do "Cowboy Take Me Away" again.

Day 8: A song that feels like the first cold day in early October and it makes you want to cry from nostalgia but also smile with hope for the future and the combination makes your arm hairs tingle—though it could just be the cooler weather doing that.

Day 9: A song that you only know about because it was featured on one of the biggest cultural influences of your generation—an *OC* mix.

Day 10: A song that you used to say you'd play at your wedding until you started questioning if getting married was ever something you would actually want to do and if you did, it probably wouldn't be the kind of wedding with traditional "wedding dances" anyway.

Day 11: A song that you loved when you were eight years old but then your dad told you it was "about cocaine" and you didn't fully understand what that meant but you weren't sure if it was okay to continue listening or not, so you stopped.

Day 12: A song that you thought was gay until you read an interview where the artist said it was about "friendship" which is, okay, fine...but still makes you like it 10% less.

Day 13: The fourth song on the burnt CD that your high school boyfriend made for you that you've somehow kept for ten years and occasionally still listen to when you lose cell service on long drives.

Day 14: A song that always makes you feel like you're in a movie and you base a whole feature film concept around this song in your mind and end up texting a pitch to your one filmmaker friend who politely says "No".

Day 15: A song you play when you're cooking dinner with your girlfriend, but you accidentally burn everything because you can't stop dancing in the kitchen.

Day 16: The third song you downloaded from Napster; before you deleted it, fearing arrest every time you saw a police car in your neighborhood.

Day 17: A Dave Matthews Band song that you've only recently (as in, in the past few weeks) started liking again and now you get sponsored Instagram ads for his winery in your stories…and honestly? You might buy the wine, too.

Day 18: A song that you posted to your Instagram story because every hot queer you knew from Tinder had posted it to theirs too, but you didn't even like it that much, you just wanted to feel a part of something bigger than yourself.

Day 19: A song by Taylor Swift about being fifteen years old that still makes you cry and cry and cry even though you are turning twenty-nine next month.

Day 20: A song by a band that you never saw live because, when it really came down to it, you wanted to stay in and watch *The Real Housewives*, but if someone were to ask you, you would say, "Oh hell yea, they're so good live."

Day 21: A different song that you suspected was about being gay and then you later find out it's true, it's a gay song! You add it to every playlist.

Day 22: A song by a band your ex loved, and you go on Spotify's "Private Session" to play the whole album while quietly reading old texts.

Day 23: A song by a band you love that you once saw your ex playing on Spotify and you wonder if they know about "Private Session" or if they wanted you to see it and feel a bit tormented by it, but then you remember your therapist saying "most people don't think about you at all," so you go take a shower or something.

Day 24: A song that mentions a place where you once lived and therefore you automatically love it, no questions asked.

Day 25: A song that the popular girls danced to at your elementary school talent show but you were not allowed to be a part of it because, "There are only 3 girls in 3LW, Emma"

Day 26: A song that your 10th-grade spring break crush played while feeling you up Panama City beach, that you later downloaded as your flip phone ringtone, to remember him by.

Day 27: A Broadway song that you actually think you could've performed someday if you'd kept doing plays past the time when you were assigned to "run lights" for the 5th-grade spring musical.

Day 28: A song from the 90s that you were absolutely too young to care about but enough Gen X men convinced you of its significance, so you end up saying things like "this band was really influential" in the place of a real opinion.

Day 29: A song that you weren't allowed to watch the music video for because it had two girls kissing, but you once saw it on every single TV screen in a Best Buy and consider this a "core memory."

Day 30: Whatever song you most wish you could see live right now but know you would spend the whole time debating whether it would be worth it to record a video or try to just live in the moment, so you end up not being able to successfully do either.

MIA

You'd never know there was a bar back here if you didn't already know there was a bar back here. I can only assume someone designed it this way. A reprieve from the bachelorette parties and craft beer enthusiasts that take over the downtown strip every weekend.

"You're going into the dumpster!" Some drunk guy yells, walking by, as I step in through the unmarked entrance in the back.

The streets are crowded, but the patio is still. Just a guy smoking a cigarette by the door next to a legal pad where you sign your name. There's one other couple at a picnic table with two beer cans in front of them.

If you sit outside, you can hear folky, acoustic covers of R&B songs, ringing out into the night from the patios of the nearby breweries. It's almost enjoyable, from that far away.

If you find yourself there at sunset, you can see a group of bats all start to circle near the horizon. A beautifully choreographed routine, ending in an ensemble dive into the chimney of some abandoned building, as if the night itself were swallowing them whole.

I have some crumpled-up dollar bills in my pocket, and it feels like a real treat. I use one for the jukebox, flipping through page after page of high school nostalgia, queuing up some old Modest Mouse songs and something sad by Songs: Ohia. The music plays, loud and full, and I smile, savoring this small act of creation.

Will cracks open a High Life before I can even say hi and slides it towards me.

"You missed her, again." He turns around to toss the cap in the recycling. "She was just here."

"High score?"

He nods.

The bar is pretty barren but has the best jukebox in the city, one pool table, and a computer screen with bar games right next to the cash register. For one dollar you can play three rounds of an old spot-the-difference game that uses dated photos from Penthouse magazines. Girls with big, 80s hair, in lingerie, sitting on motorcycles or in bathtubs. The "differences" are rarely on their bodies, which sit garishly at the forefront of the image, but in the tiles of the tub or the mirrors of the motorcycle. It's the kind of thing that makes you feel smart and stupid at the same time.

"Damn," I say, taking a foamy sip of the beer. "Did she play?"

Will kind of laughs, "Oh yeah. Beat her own top score, I think."

I touch the machine, lighting it up.

"See for yourself." Will disappears into the back just as the second Modest Mouse song comes on, for no one but me.

I slide a crumpled bill into the machine and press the button for Erotic Photo Hunt.

Usually, I can make it pretty far before the timer turns red and my three precious clues have run dry. I've learned that a bra strap is often slipped over a shoulder. I know to count light fixtures, earrings, and fence posts. Tapping the first few, pretty easily and eventually finding the last remaining difference—but not without a clench in my chest. The fear that it's over. That I've failed.

I almost beat her once. I got the third-highest score, causing a ripple in her clean sweep of the scoreboard. For one night and one night only, it read:

MIA

MIA

ADH

MIA

MIA

MIA

MIA

MIA

I felt like a real champion, seeing my initials up there with her name. The Michael Jordan of Erotic Photo Hunt. The Tiger Woods of Megatouch.

MIA got her highest score yet, the next day. She played until I was off the map entirely.

"Works nearby, I think," Will said when I saw what she had done. He spoke a bit louder, over "Farewell Transmission" blaring from the jukebox. "She doesn't talk much, keeps to herself."

I nod.

"Mostly just comes in after her shift, puts some dollars in, and leaves."

I play a round and lose earlier than I anticipate; thrown off by a fold of fabric under a blonde with the biggest boobs I've ever seen. She's probably my mom's age now—a thought I quickly push away.

The screen lights up with GAME OVER and then shows me the new score sitting at the top of the board next to MIA.

1,009,816.

"Holy shit," I say to Will. He raises his eyebrows, wiping the inside of a pint glass with a tattered rag. She's done it. She's crossed the million-point threshold.

I wonder if this even means anything to her. While I sit here most nights, playing against this elusive stranger, she's simply trying to be better than she was the night before. ADH—my letters—mean nothing to her. I'm not a threat or even healthy competition. I'm nobody.

I play my next round—a brunette with a pixie cut laying spread eagle by a pool. I spot all five differences, easy. Next, an older woman with an updo, draped in a leopard print robe in front of a jacuzzi. This one is a bit trickier, but I get the job done.

I watch, nervously, as my points rise. Will I get close to her high score? Make it back onto the scoreboard, tucked somewhere amidst her unrelenting glory?

A group of loud, rowdy friends enter the bar, laughing.

I turn around, briefly wondering if it's MIA, back for another win. I imagine what she looks like. Have I seen her before, unknowingly? Perhaps we go to the same grocery store or get our coffees from the same scowling, young barista. If it was in fact her, would I shake her hand? Step aside and let her play?

A flash from the game pulls me back. The timer's running out. I've wasted precious seconds on a bunch of what-ifs. I tap frantically, using my last clue on a maddeningly subtle difference hidden in some trees. It's too late. Game Over. I reflexively let my fist hit the bar. I think *next time.*

"What is this shit?" One of the newcomers says, gesturing vaguely at the air, but referring to the music. My music.

"Hey did y'all sign in," the man at the door steps inside, but only barely. He leaves his lit cigarette in his mouth, burning orange from under his mustache. "Get back out here." He points at his yellow legal pad.

It's almost too easy to tell who belongs here and who doesn't.

The one who hates good music rolls her eyes. "Oh, okayyy." She walks back outside. "Calm down."

The mustache man doesn't like this and asks the group where they live. "Tourists aren't welcome." but they're already retreating, laughter mixing with muttered complaints. I can almost see the one-star Yelp review taking shape in their minds.

As the door swings shut, the familiar silence settles back in. I turn to the game, aware that I've got one more round before my dollar runs out. Do I call it quits? Come back tomorrow after some sleep? Or maybe I need another beer.

I'm feeling drunk already, but someone once said crossing your eyes helps you spot differences faster. Sounds like bullshit, but I'd try anything.

"Hey, Will," I call out, the thought suddenly striking me as hilarious. "You think MIA crosses her eyes when she plays?"

Will doesn't even look up from the glass he's wiping. "What? I don't know, man."

I press the button and let a new sultry image wash over me. Full vagina, which is rare. I tap and tap again. Three more. The timer moves from green to yellow and I hold my breath. Tap.

"Hey."

A voice from behind me, soft and confident, as the timer fades to red.

Tap.

"I think I left my ID here."

Will shakes his head without looking up from wiping down glasses. "Nothing's turned up"

Tap. I sigh. I've made it to the next round.

She lingers for a moment, glancing around the empty room. My chest tightens as her eyes skim past the game.

"Excuse me." She's talking to me now.

I turn, the game forgotten. She looks... hopeful? Nervous?

"Are you..." She hesitates, then carefully enunciates each letter. "M-I-A?"

I shake my head.

"Oh." Disappointment flashes across her face. "Sorry to bother you."

She turns to leave. I consider saying something—about our shared quest, or maybe just my own name—but the words stick in my throat.

The door creaks shut behind her. I stare at it, then at the Megatouch screen. GAME OVER flashes mockingly.

I turn back to the game, finger hovering over START. For the first time, I hesitate.

UR SUCH AN INSPIRATION

"Ur such an inspiration" was the last comment Avery received on her blog. She'd stopped posting altogether for three weeks, up until the final entry. Her longest break in years. Avery's admission that she wasn't doing well drew a wave of support—countless tiny avatars leaving words of encouragement. But she could see through it.

The purpose of recovery blogging wasn't to get better; it was to stay just thin enough to look like you're trying. To post meals that looked complex enough to make a starving person jealous, all while staying thin enough to do the same. She'd gotten away with it for a while. But, of course, it couldn't go on forever.

The rules in the center were different. She had to eat. A lot. No one cared that she was mildly famous in the world of recovery bloggers. In fact, no one knew who she was at all. She had gotten so used to the little online world she had built, it was jarring to realize there were other sick people out there. Real people.

"Avery." She looked up from her bowl of spaghetti. "Avery, it's your turn."

The other residents often played games at the table to distract themselves.

"What letter are we on?" Avery asked, picking up her fork and swirling it around. Catherine, the loudest of the bunch, groaned.

"You're always messing us up. We're on D."

"Oh." Avery's mind raced to her favorite band. "Death Cab for Cutie."

The woman to her left was new and looked to be in her forties, though you could never really tell. She'd arrived this morning, straight from a hospital stay, with a giant suitcase that had been wheeled into Avery's room. She'd be Avery's third roommate in fifty-five days.

"The Eagles," the woman said, darting her eyes around for approval. "Eagles."

"That counts, that counts," Catherine affirmed.

Avery took a bite of spaghetti. It was room temperature and piled high with ground beef and shredded cheese. She'd eaten this meal once a week since she'd arrived, and it never got any better.

During meals, she often wondered what her sister was eating back at home. Delicata squash with goat cheese. Persimmons and granola. Fresh arugula. Meanwhile, her fork pushed around lukewarm noodles. She sometimes resented becoming the sicker one, the one uprooted from her life and forced into health. It didn't seem fair.

"It'll be good for you to spend some time apart." Avery's mother had said, sitting on her bed, explaining the decision that was made without her. "We can help Jane here." Avery wrapped her arms around her kneecaps, letting the implication that her parents couldn't help her, linger.

Jane and Avery had done everything together for as long as she could remember. Gymnastics, choir, community college—even their blogs were created on the same day. They'd comment on each other's posts of identical meals and outfits, getting sick and better together so many times; Avery thought the cycle would last forever.

Something changed a few months before Avery entered the center. Avery's meals grew smaller and more sporadic. Jane met some friends in her Pottery elective; the only class they didn't share. Jane began to post on her blog about nights out with new friends, and movies she'd seen. Occasionally, she'd upload photos of her breakfast and muse on food and recovery, but as her social life picked up, she started posting less and less. She began looking at Avery with a certain sadness, instead of the usual blend of comradery and competition. This shift pushed Avery deeper into isolation. *Fine*, she thought, *I'll be the sick twin. I'll excel at that.*

"Mail time," Nurse Debbie said when the empty plates were cleared. Everyone had to wait one hour in the common room after dinner before they could go back to their rooms. Nurse Debbie shuffled through a stack of envelopes and walked around, plopping them next to the recipients.

Avery had left the name of the center in her final blog post and occasionally received mail from people she'd never met. The letters were mostly encouraging, offering vague platitudes of support and optimism. When the other residents would ask who the letters were from Avery would say "friends" and sometimes she'd even believe it. Just letters from my friends. But these were strangers, faceless usernames who only knew her curated online persona.

Nurse Debbie set two envelopes beside Avery on the couch that she was sharing with Catherine. Catherine had started knitting, a common pastime in the center, and was talking to anyone who would listen about how her parents were coming for Family Weekend. It would be their first time in Tennessee.

The first letter Avery received was from someone named Kara who had written their Blogspot username in parenthesis. Kara (thelittleturnip). The envelope was covered in glittery cupcake stickers. Avery tucked it behind the second envelope. One from Jane. Her fingers lingered on the familiar handwriting.

Dearest Avery,

I miss you so much!! I was walking around campus today thinking about how I wish you were here with me. It just got cold out and finally feels like fall. Mom says we might be coming next weekend for Family Weekend! I really need to study for my midterms but I sort of feel like... fuck 'em, you know? I hope you are eating lots of delicious things and meeting some cool people. Everyone keeps commenting on my blog (and yours, too), asking about you and I tell them you are doing well. You are, right? Do you remember, when we were kids and we'd sleep in the bunk beds at Gram's house and read Babysitters Club books and count the daddy long legs on the walls? And how we'd play orphanage, and you would always make me be the orphan?? I was trying to explain this to Brooke today. Maybe if you are home by November 2nd you can go to the Iron & Wine concert with us. Ok, I have to go study, but I miss you so much and am sending the biggest hug.

XOXO, Jane.

Avery folded the letter and tucked it into her pocket, but she kept the thelittleturnip's letter sealed. When she was back in her room, she'd put it in the pile with all the others. She liked to save them for days when she was feeling especially down and then read them all at once, feeling the same familiar rush of serotonin that she used to get from publishing a new blog entry and watching the comments roll in.

"I'm Betsy," The new resident said, once they'd finally been released to their rooms. She was unpacking her suitcase on the bed next to Avery's. One tiny pair of sweatpants after the other.

"Avery."

Avery spent most of her nights reading from a list of pre-approved books that were allowed in the center and ignoring everyone. When she first arrived, she tried to make friends and speak up in group therapy. She would chat with her first roommate late into the night. She thought that having a positive attitude would get her out faster, but as she geared up to begin her eighth week, she had given up hope that she had any control over her length of her stay.

"I thought so," Betsy said, zipping up her now empty suitcase. "Jane's twin."

Avery looked up. "Who told you that?"

"You did. Well, you both did." She sat down on the bed, warmly. "I read your blogs."

"Your post, the one about space. Fighting for space in the womb." Betsy stood and began pinning a handful of photos printed on computer paper onto their shared bulletin board. "And now, trying to take up as little space as possible." She didn't notice Avery growing increasingly uncomfortable, her fingers unconsciously tracing the outline of Jane's letter in her pocket. "That one was really beautiful."

⧖

Avery's therapist, whom she met with twice a week, would often tell her that she needed to open up more. They talked endlessly about vulnerability and how honesty builds connection. Avery never felt the need to make friends growing up because she'd always had Jane. When she discovered blogging, she felt comforted by the distance the screen provided. The only place Avery felt she could truly be vulnerable was online.

"I think you need to participate in Family Weekend," Avery's therapist, Carly, said, sitting across from Avery in her office. They were reaching the end of their weekly session. "It could really prove to us that you've made progress here."

Avery stared at the ugly painting of the Eiffel Tower that hung behind her therapist. Carly's office smelled like Bath and Body Works and had the biggest window in the whole place; something that didn't seem particularly fair. Avery would've loved a window in her room.

"Jane says she's coming," Avery said. "I *am* participating."

Family Weekend happened once a month and this would be Avery's second. She watched, last time, as parents and siblings, husbands and wives, gathered in the lobby of the center for snacks and conversation. Eventually, two families went into the center of a circle of chairs and took part in a public family therapy session. The idea was to model healthy communication—to show how well the treatment center could work. The thought of it felt demeaning to Avery. A violation of whatever loose threads of trust she'd worked to establish with Carly and with this whole place.

"I think you and Jane should go in the center of the circle, this time," Carly said, folding her hands together on her lap. Her fingernails were bright red and looked like hard plastic. "I bet you'd gain a lot from it. You'd be such an inspiration for the newer girls."

The words from her last blog comment flashed in Avery's mind: ur such an inspiration. She fixated on her feet, watching them tap together, then apart. An inspiration was the last thing she wanted to be. She really just wanted to be home. The concept of "getting better"' felt foreign and almost repulsive. For now, she could play along.

Shifting uncomfortably, Avery tucked her hands beneath her thighs.

"Just think about it," Carly said in an overly gentle way that made Avery's skin crawl. "You can let me know."

That night, after a shower, Avery sat on her bed and read through her letters.

Avery,
I know you don't know me, but I feel like I know you.

Avery,
I've been reading your blog since 2010 (two whole years!)

Avery,
I was so sad to see that you were struggling.

Avery,
You've inspired me to push myself, too.

Avery,
I know recovery isn't easy but I believe in you!!

Xoxo,
Katie (happyhealthydreamer)

All the best,
Becca (butterrflyygal)

<3
Kara (thelittleturnip)

Lots of love!!!!
C (livingfreeee)

sending hugs,
Amy (gettingbetterthanever)

⧗

Avery was often the first one awake in the unit. She hated standing in line for vitals and the later you emerged from your room, the longer you had to wait. She stood on the scale with her back to the numbers, as she'd done every morning for the past fifty-six days.

Nurse Debbie wrapped a blood pressure cuff around her arm and scribbled something on her chart. She skimmed over Avery's information and then looked up in surprise, meeting Avery's stare. Nurse Debbie smiled.

"Happy birthday."

Avery and Jane had never spent a single birthday apart. She never expected her twenty-first would consist of force-feeding herself pancakes and scrambled eggs before a group therapy session where she'd listen to Catherine go on and on about body image and her new stepmom—the same things she always talked about.

She imagined Jane putting on a cute, sparkly skirt, going out for cocktails with her Pottery class friends and taking photos for her blog. Maybe their parents even put balloons in her room, just like they had done when they were kids.

Nurse Debbie let Avery play whatever music she wanted on the iPod mini that was hooked up to a small speaker in the room where they ate meals. She took her time spinning the little wheel, going through the library of songs one of the nurse techs had downloaded before selecting a Nick Drake album.

"This is painfully depressing," Catherine said, halfway through the meal. "Just when I thought this place couldn't get any sadder."

After breakfast, as everyone took their requisite empty plates to the cart by the door, Nurse Debbie said, "Hey Avery," in a quiet, gentle tone. "I have a surprise for you."

Avery followed Nurse Debbie down the hallway to the locked office that had a computer and desk inside. Computer privileges were the hardest privilege to obtain. In her entire stay, she'd only seen one resident gain access. The resident had been pulled aside, just like Avery, and emerged to the main room an hour later, blissed out on emails and Facebook wall posts.

"Go on," Nurse Debbie said, gesturing through the now open door.

Avery thanked the nurse and stepped inside, sitting down on the large, black computer chair and sinking into its worn leather.

She did a single spin before logging onto Facebook, where predictably there was a slew of "happy birthday" notifications from people she only ever heard from on this day, once a year. People who were friends with her parents, people she knew from grade school. Her profile picture was of her and Jane from a photoshoot they'd done with the self-timer on her digital camera. They were standing outside, near a creek, wearing white dresses and lace-up boots. "This would be our album cover," Jane had said after the shutter snapped. Avery barely recognized herself.

The cheerful messages felt hollow. Seeking something more familiar, she closed out of Facebook and logged onto Blogspot. There was an overwhelming number of new entries from the other bloggers she followed.

what i ate today

what i wore today

Struggling.

*sigh*sigh*sigh*sigh*

Change…

things are looking up

The latest was entitled BIRTHDAY from Jane.

hey girlies ~

tomorrow is my BIRTHDAY. the big 2-1. finally. i'm planning to go out for breakfast with my mom before class and then to the art museum with two friends from school. we'll probably go out for drinks afterward bc i can do that now hehe. well, not now, but tomorrow. i'm excited but i'm also feeling sad. this will be my first birthday without avery (my twin, most of u kno lol) and i wish more than anything we could celebrate together. but im proud of her and know we will have the most amazing 22nd birthday eating cake and drinking champagne next year. i also think this will be my last post on this blog. i've loved getting to share my recovery and my food and art with you all but i feel so busy between school and classes and friends, now. i'm also in such a good place w food and my body and keep forgetting to photograph things etc. mostly just ready to move on and liveeee my lifeeeee. add me on facebook if you want to stay connected! maybe i'll still check back in on occasion.

love you all <3 <3 <3

The post ended with a photo of Jane, taken on her digital camera. It was black and white, and she had cat-eye eyeliner and a pouty face. There were sixty-two comments.

Avery scrolled through them, hurriedly. Most said versions of the same things. Happy Birthday! Good Luck! So proud of you! Avery clicked leave a comment and stared at the blinking cursor until her vision began to blur. Jane's post loomed above—a farewell to their shared online world, a declaration of health and normalcy that Avery couldn't match.

Avery typed out *"miss you, janie"* and then deleted it. Carefully—slow with each press of the backspace. It wasn't enough.

She logged out and walked back into the main room, with the others. Catherine was knitting on the couch, one leg tucked beneath her. Avery sat down beside her and quietly, out of the corner of her mouth, Catherine whispered, "Lucky you."

⧖

As Family Weekend approached, a noticeable unease spread through the center.

"I'm excited to see my dad but nervous to see my stepmom," Catherine said, tearfully, in group therapy. Most of the other residents looked bored and zoned out but Carly looked at Catherine attentively.

"Where do you think those feelings are coming from?" Carly asked, in a milky, sweet voice.

"Probably from how I used to feel around her back home. She was always dieting and talking about her weight. Like she was competing with me."

Carly nodded. An empathetic performance that Avery had grown used to.

"I just know that she'll see me now and feel," Catherine looked up, shuffling her feet. "I don't know…like she's winning."

"And you don't want her to win."

Catherine shook her head.

"Do you feel competition with her in other ways?"

Avery stifled an eye roll. She knew that the answer was yes and that the competition was for Catherine's father's attention. How many times would they have a version of this same conversation? She stared out the one tiny window of the group therapy room at a man riding a lawn mower in the distance. She imagined trading places with him and driving the lawn mower miles and miles away to somewhere else. Anywhere else.

"Avery, how are you feeling about this weekend?" Carly asked, jolting Avery away from her fantasy and back inside the room.

"I feel fine."

There was silence. "Fine" was rarely an acceptable adjective, here.

"I, um," She stumbled, realizing she hadn't escaped. "I'm excited to see Jane."

"Are there any other feelings coming up?"

Avery shook her head. "I just hope it feels," she looked down at her hands, one picking at the nail of the other, seemingly without her permission.

"Normal." She looked up. "Like nothing's changed."

⧗

Avery placed the letter on her dresser, atop a dwindling pile. With Jane moving on from blogging and Avery locked up in the center, they were most certainly becoming irrelevant online. Soon the letters would stop altogether. Avery fell back onto her bed, wishing the thought didn't bother her so much. Sure, she could move on, too. She could start taking a new class, make friends, find something to care about that wasn't on a plate or a screen. Avery stared at the ceiling, wondering when she'd forgotten how to do any of that.

Betsy emerged from the bathroom, oblivious, with a towel wrapped around her head and her body.

"I can't believe you and Jane are doing the circle thing, tomorrow." She said, sitting down on the other bed. "It's like…celebrity therapy."

Avery rolled over onto her side, looking at Betsy with a slight eye roll. "Please." She knew Betsy was making a joke, but she took a moment to revel in the prestige.

Avery couldn't remember the last time she'd seen her reflection. Her hair, she knew, was a tangled mess, perpetually bundled atop her head. Would Jane see her and immediately feel thankful that it was Avery in the center and not her? Avery used to feel so pleased by being the sickest. A feeble badge of honor. Avery closed her eyes, unsure if she was more afraid of Jane's pity or of her relief.

⌛

Jane was quiet when she arrived at the center. She held onto a plastic cup of fruit punch, for comfort, but didn't take a sip. Maybe she was scared that with one wrong move, they'd take her in, too. Trade one twin out for the other.

Jane watched the other families give out hugs while she looked around for Avery. She felt nervous, wondering if Avery would be a whole new person. Jane considered if she, too, was a new person in Avery's absence. She didn't know for sure.

Avery finally emerged from behind a closed door wearing sweatpants and a t-shirt from a high school choir trip they'd both attended. Jane wondered, briefly, if that was actually her shirt on Avery's new body.

"You look great," Jane said.

"Don't lie."

Avery was relieved to see her sister. For a moment as they stood in front of each other, it felt like they weren't in a treatment center. It felt like they were back at home, taking digital camera photos and writing on their blogs; going on long neighborhood walks, discussing dream-like futures both of them were too scared to reach for.

In the center of the room, a circle of empty chairs waited. Plastic and unyielding. There, they would sit and perform recovery again, this time without the veil of a screen.

A chair scraped against linoleum as someone sat down. Then another. And another.

Jane's breath hitched and Avery's eyes darted to the door.

Outside, sunlight spilled across the asphalt. Wind rustled the leaves of a distant tree. It had been fifty-eight days in this same building. Avery remembered what the sunlight first felt like, once she'd been cleared for a daily, fifteen-minute walk. Glorious and pitiful.

Avery leaned close, her whisper barely audible. "I can't." She eyed the open door, with that same sun blasting through, and a shuffle of bodies they could easily get lost in.

Jane's response was immediate. "Me neither."

Avery's grip tightened and the room zoomed out around them. "Come on."

Jane dropped her fruit punch to the ground, and hand-in-hand, they ran.

They ran past Carly, her clipboard clattering to the floor. They ran past the man on the lawn mower, who seemed frozen in time, the grass clippings suspended in the air around him. The busy street was eerily empty of cars, and their footsteps echoed loud on the pavement.

They ran past the strip of fast-food restaurants and abandoned storefronts. Avery's legs burned, unused to such exertion. They ran and ran until they were at least a mile away, near a school with an empty playground.

The twins tumbled together onto the asphalt, coughing and giggling. High off adrenaline and freedom, far away from everything except each other.

⌛

Avery returned to her room that night in a trance.

She was so used to going through the motions. Breakfast, snack, lunch, snack, dinner, snack. She felt like a robot. She felt nothing.

Betsy looked to Avery, sympathetically. "Sorry, she didn't show, Avery."

Avery diverted her eyes. "It's fine."

She hated the way Betsy looked at her. Like she knew everything when she really knew nothing. So, she had read some blog posts, so what?

"Jane told me that she had midterms and stuff." Avery reached for her sweatshirt. "It's not a big deal. We're going to go to an Iron & Wine show, once I'm out of here."

Tonight's night snack had been yogurt with granola and a peach. Avery had choked her way through it. She said "pass" when it was her turn to name a movie that started with the letter G. Everyone let her, even Catherine.

Avery blinked, the last wisps of fantasy fading, and opened a book from her top shelf, one that sat neatly beneath her stack of fan letters. She pushed them to the side, crawled under the covers, and read until she fell asleep.

THE CANNONBALLER'S DAUGHTER

They shoot a man out of a cannon every year at eight p.m. at the Mountain State Fair. He says his daddy did it first—broke all the records and taught him how. Now his daughter Chloe, barely seventeen, stands at the cannon's base beaming up at him.

A crowd has gathered. Teens in cropped shirts under flannels holding cotton candies, and kids lugging large stuffed animals that their parents surely won for them. We got here ten minutes early and stand around, shuffling on the sides of our tennis shoes.

Reagan takes a sip of lemonade from a plastic souvenir cup. "You think he ever gets hurt? Misses the net?"

The man gives a bellowing, echo-y speech, thanking the troops before he climbs into the cannon.

I swallow. "I don't think he'd be here if he missed the net."

Chloe, the human cannonball heir, darts around the base, adjusting, checking and then rechecking. She's quick and precise. Watching her, I think she might have the toughest job of all.

The opening of the cannon, painted bright with cartoon flames, points toward the sky. Reagan's hand finds mine, squeezing tight as the countdown starts. "I can't look," they whisper.

A kid barely old enough to walk puts his hands to his ears in anticipation and turns into his mother's legs. *Three, two.* I feel Reagan's face burrow into my shoulder. *One!*

With a thunderous crack, Chloe fires the cannon. Her father flies out, headfirst and arrow-straight. He clears the Ferris wheel before arching back down towards the earth. I watch as couples, dangling from little buckets in the sky, strain their necks to follow him. He tucks his chin and forward-rolls into the net with grace, as people cheer.

I look to Chloe and watch her shoulders soften.

Reagan jumps up and down, pretending they saw the whole thing. "That was incredible!" I take the cup out of their hand and slide the straw up and down, finding a perfect spot between the ice cubes to slurp up the final, sweet drops.

"Let's go look at the quilts."

My mom's quilt got a second-place ribbon in the adult category. Her "Paris" theme features a fabric Eiffel Tower right in the center. She's never even left the state.

"It's nice," Reagan says, reaching up to touch the hemmed edge, despite the "No Touching" signs hanging everywhere.

"She doesn't really think so." I look at the first-place quilt. 2019 Best in Show. "She thinks hers shoulda got first." The winning quilt's theme was "Family Tree". There's a big branchy oak at the center and symbols representing real people at the edges. A book, some skates. Things each person in this quilter's family probably loves.

"Well," Reagan's voice echoes in the near-empty showroom. "There's always next year."

The expo center is quiet and spacious, compared to the energy beyond its doors. I can hear each of Reagan's footsteps as we walk through the aisles, admiring the large, bulbous squash, glossy peppers, and silly, biblical dioramas made by other teenagers. Reagan is touching everything with a casual coolness that I can't help but be jealous of.

As we round a corner towards the embroidery section, Reagan's hand grabs my shoulder.

"There's Chloe."

We stop and I look up to see the cannonballer's daughter admiring a smock dress with a third-place ribbon attached to it. She's taller than she looked at the base of the cannon, clutching a bare cotton candy stick—a paper white cone coated in crusted blue sugar. She sees us and smiles with a slight wave.

"Nice work out there," Reagan says with a bit of a nervous croak, which surprises me. Their voice carries awkwardly across the expo center.

"Please," Chloe's gaze drops to her flip-flops. Her voice is sweet and natural. "I'm not the one soaring through the sky."

"You want to be?" I find myself asking.

"Someday." Chloe leans against the table, her cotton candy stick hovering dangerously close to the prize-winning dress. She doesn't seem to notice. "Once Daddy gets too old."

Reagan's fingers drift over the dress's hem.

"I like this," they say softly, admiring the intricate embroidery.

Chloe tilts her head, curiously. Everyone's always so careful around here about what they can like.

My mom never taught me how to quilt, even though I asked. Even though quilting is something she calls a "family tradition". I offered my help with the Eiffel Tower quilt, and she sent me to the library to print out pictures of Paris from Google images. I wanted to feel the fabric in my hands, to guide the needle and thread. I wanted to sew.

"Are you guys from around here?" Chloe asks, finally tossing her cone into a nearby trash can.

"Close by," Reagan says, gesturing to nowhere. "Next town over."

Chloe explains that she's from Michigan but tours all over, firing her dad out of the cannon her grandpa built. Nashville is her favorite. "If I wasn't already gonna be a human cannonball, I'd be a country star."

"Have you ever been to Paris?" I ask, thinking of my mom's quilt a few rows over. Her second-place dream.

"I've been to Paris, Tennessee." She giggles, revealing shiny, bright blue braces across her teeth. "Not quite the same."

Chloe, Reagan, and I walk to the back of a line that has formed for the chair lifts that take you over the whole Mountain State Fair in a colorful bucket. The line is long, so I agree to hold our spot while Reagan gets ribbon fries from the yellow, steaming stand nearby.

"Pass," Chloe says when asked if she wants anything. "I get so sick of all the fair food."

With Reagan gone, I feel an immediate discomfort that Chloe doesn't seem to notice.

"Is that your boyfriend?" She nods in the direction of Reagan's retreating figure. I shake my head and kind of laugh.

"Best friend."

"Cute."

Chloe is towering and gangly and all I can think about is her body being flung several hundred feet in the air above us. A shooting country star.

I watch Reagan out of the corner of my eye. They wear everything so easily—lipstick, nail polish, certainty.

I blurt, "Do you get scared... doing that?"

She looks confused.

"Shooting your dad out of the cannon?"

We move up in line, sidestepping some younger kids who are pushing each other, unaware of their bodies in space.

"You get used to it."

She tells me that he broke his back once when she was twelve. She wasn't the one firing him off though, thank God. Says she'd probably never get over it, if she had been.

"Daddy was worried I wouldn't be a daredevil when I was born. Probably wishing for a boy or something." I nod, still thinking about my mother's quilt and the sewing lessons I never received. She would've sat with me and showed me patterns and techniques, had I been born someone else. "But I don't really get scared." She looks upward and shrugs. "So, I guess he lucked out."

Reagan returns, happily munching on from a thin, almost translucent bag of fries. "Ya gotta try these."

I take a handful and shove them in my mouth, rubbing my salty fingertips onto my pants as I chew.

From the sky, we can see everything. Every light and every body, moving together, slowly on the ground below. The kiddie tilt-a-whirl spins at a gentle pace, while its bigger, faster cousin whirls nearby. The Ferris wheel creaks through its rotation, pausing just often enough to spoil any dreams of a cinematic moment at the top. Every food stand pulses with competing bright colors and increasingly hyperbolic signs. *Funnel cakes! Turkey legs!!! Cotton candy!!!!!*

The chair lift moves slowly, but the way my feet are dangling into the dark night air, makes me feel kinda nauseous.

"You're scared," Reagan says, grabbing onto my thigh and grinning. They've taken the middle seat. Chloe seems almost bored, as if she's seen it all before. Every town, every fair. Every sky.

"Well, if we fell from here, we'd be goners."

Reagan drops a fry and watches its slow descent back down to earth. The wind gives it a moment of desperate flight before gravity ultimately wins.

"Maybe not."

On the drive home, when I close my eyes, I feel like I'm still on a carnival ride. Seasick and floaty. I see the fair lights, bright behind my eyelids.

Reagan stays over at my house, and they won't stop going on about Chloe. "I bet she could be a country star if she wanted." We share a bed, topped with one of grandmother's quilts. Maybe it was a prize winner at the Mountain State Fair, long ago, or maybe it was just something she made to keep her warm. "She's really got that look, you know?" I nod, yes. She's got that look.

I keep my eyes closed until the afterlight finally fades.

HOW-TO-WATER-
THE-PLANTS

Zoey made out with the wall of the student gallery space for one hour, as her painting final. She was wearing bright red lipstick. No one was there when she did it because the art wasn't so much the act of kissing the wall but the smudges left behind. The way you could tell that she had done it.

An hour seemed like an awfully long time.

I tried to imagine it, thinking about the way the walls of that gallery must feel, painted over in stark white paint every couple of months once a new show goes up. Scratchy and storied.

I sort of didn't believe her—that she did it for a whole hour. But there was no way to prove otherwise.

A single spotlight shone on her lip prints, which were messy but implied that she had a rhythm when she kissed. This was something I wondered if I had. A pattern, a direction. I guess so much of that depends on who is kissing you back—something Zoey didn't need to worry about with the wall.

I wonder where she put her hands.

I always struggle with where mine should go. When I'm caught up in the moment and not overthinking, they naturally find their way to the back of someone's neck, gently tugging at their hair. If I am thinking about it too much, I forget to use them entirely. Or maybe they go around someone's whole body in an awkward hug shape. Something very un-sexy.

I imagine Zoey touching herself as she kissed the wall, hands up and down her own torso.

I imagine Zoey's hands clasped sweetly behind her back, out of the way.

If I had been in her critique, I would have asked none of these questions. Instead, I would have said something like, "The juxtaposition of intimacy and sterility is quite compelling." And then I would have gone home and kissed my own walls, just to see.

My final painting class was last semester since I decided to switch my major over to Graphic Design. No one was making out with walls in design classes, but people still found ways to be shocking. Blank pages taped to the wall, followed by an overly profound explanation, and my professor ending class early, saying, "If you want to give a middle finger to the program, just do that and don't waste my time."

I'm looking at Zoey's lipstick on the wall before my typography class because the gallery space is downstairs underneath the computer studios, and I am chronically early to things, even though I wish I wasn't. It's quiet in the gallery, and my backpack keychains make wind chime-like noises with each step I take.

I wonder how her piece was received in critique. Did they talk about the futility of human connection? The eroticism of architecture? Or did someone just say, "Cool," and move on to the next piece? Art school is full of these small heartbreaks.

I often think one thing about the work we present and then change my mind once we talk about it collectively. Some people have very boring-looking projects but very convincing stories about them. I almost believed in the blank pages—in their merit, in their integrity.

I'm not really friends with Zoey, though we are friends on Facebook and, more recently, Tumblr. I don't have her number, and we never really hang out, outside of class. She reblogs a lot of stuff about anime. She loves *Sailor Moon*. Everyone likes her in art school. She seems easy to like.

My own Tumblr is much more aspirational—like I'm really trying to express a certain vibe, that I don't actually possess. I reblog photos of Winona Ryder looking sad in the 90s. Aesthetically delicate breakfast spreads. Selfies, taken on my laptop's photo booth app where my hair is sweeping sideways, tucking behind my ear, and revealing the eyebrow ring I got on the day of the break-up.

My ex has a blog called how-to-water-the-plants. Just like that, with the dashes in between each word.

I try not to look at it anymore, but sometimes I pour a third glass of wine and type in the URL, just to see pictures of their dog or their new haircut. Light-filled rooms I used to once be in with them.

When I would make out with them, my hands would always do the hair thing instead of the hug thing.

In typography, we are designing our own typefaces, which has me thinking about letters more deeply than ever before. The relationship between each shape. A small system. You can create any letter once you've figured out just a few simple forms.

It's an intricate process involving lots of measurements and rulers. Sometimes, I think I would rather just make out with the wall, but the precision is soothing in a different way. Every letter, forever the same. There are no surprises.

`how-to-water-the-plants` used to take a marker and write notes to me on their bathroom mirror. They were always writing by hand, leaving letters and poems scattered around their room. Without meaning to, I've studied the ways their t's and h's connect in "the" and "there". The loopy, lowercase f's they use.

"Beautiful, I'm going to read all your favorite books." and *"p.s. eat the garden tomato."*

The last 'o' barely hanging onto the rest of the word, as if it was surprised to be included.

I used to take pictures of the notes and post them to my Tumblr. I'd step out of the shower, steam covering the mirror, with my phone in hand, the faint, pale outline of my naked body behind the words.

When I think back on the photo, I think about it as if I am presenting it to my classmates in critique. Maybe we would discuss presence and absence, *blah, blah, blah*. How viewing the note is like viewing Zoey's lipstick stains right now. Someone was here, and now they are not.

Zoey and her friends enter the gallery loudly, holding Chick-fil-A cups from the campus dining hall. Their presence is startling. Harsh and lively, compared to my contemplative silence. I'm sure, for them, the noise level is natural, if not slightly subdued. A continuation of whatever lunch conversation they'd been having. The voices collectively fall as they become more aware—when they see me hovering.

I hate that whenever I see Zoey now, I imagine what it's like to kiss her.

This is the power of art. I think, jokingly, in my head. And then, *No, this is the power of your closeted homosexuality.*

I never told anyone about or how my hands always knew what to do. I didn't have enough Tumblr followers for anyone to wonder where the mirror notes came from. There was no gallery spotlight on my lip prints.

I felt relieved when the relationship ended, and I didn't have to feel like a liar anymore. I felt lost.

The kid with the blank pages and the hot head once asked our professor, "How can you even express yourself as a designer? How do you rationalize typography as art?" He said the word "typography" with a certain disdain.

Questioning the legitimacy of graphic design happens all the time when you're surrounded by painters and sculptors—the jocks of the art degrees. People who likely know they will struggle in the "real world" but are on top for now, in the confines of art school. They view art as pure and design as selling out. I don't think they're wrong, but I've never had much conviction in my opinions.

"You are solving a problem," my professor said, calmly. "Put yourself into the answer, as best you can, but ultimately, you better solve the problem."

Could I express my feeling of loss in a typeface? Perhaps in the ways my t's never touch my h's. They reach out longingly, but there is distance. Calculated and consistent. Could I make them feel like they want to touch?

I linger by a photo installation, feigning purpose, while Zoey and her friends crowd around her piece. They measure themselves against her lip prints, snapping photos. Two of them kiss for the camera—I hear only silence, then shrill laughter. "Let me see, let me see!" More laughter.

Someone hits the lights as they leave—a habit, maybe. My eyes bloom with phantom colors, adjusting to the sudden darkness. I try not to bump anything on my way out.

PRAYER BREAKFAST

knew that downloading music was illegal, but my dad was the one who showed me how to do it, so I didn't worry too much. I still prayed at night for God to forgive me, just in case.

>

The Australian's username was koala_rocks47 and he was twenty-six.

I was eleven and three-quarters. I'd found the John Mayer fan forum through a Google search after Drew read the lyrics to "Why Georgia" in Literature class, during our poetry unit.

"Am I living it right?" Over and over again, while his hands shook.

I wasn't living at all, not really. Not until I heard that song.

>

koala_rocks47: hey Why_GeorgiaGurl! saw ur post about wanting the Melbourne bootleg. I've got the whole show, soundboard quality. want me to upload it for you?

Why_GeorgiaGurl: omg yes please!!! I only have the first 4 songs from limewire and they keep cutting out

koala_rocks47: no worries, mate. us hardcore fans gotta stick together. btw love your username - georgia's my favorite track too. how old are you?

Why_GeorgiaGurl: 16

>

On Wednesday mornings, Pastor Jim drove the Presbyterian middle schoolers to Bojangles on Cleveland Highway. We called it Prayer Breakfast.

At Bojangles, I would order a cinnamon biscuit, a buttered biscuit, and a Mr. Pibb. I'd watch Drew across the restaurant while Jim asked us about our "faith journeys."

"Anyone want to share what God's been doing in their lives this week?"

I could've shared that I'd stayed up until three a.m. downloading bootlegs with someone named koala_rocks47, who thinks I am in high school. Instead, I said nothing and watched Drew's headphones settle around his neck, wondering what holy music played through them.

Last week on the bus, his batteries died and he asked to share mine. We listened to a live John Mayer show from Melbourne together. During "Comfortable" our arms touched and stayed touching for three whole songs.

"Where do you find all these?" he asked.

"The internet," I said.

>

The next Wednesday his batteries worked but he asked to share headphones anyway. This time he played me Damien Rice and said "This will make you cry," and I pretended it did even though I was mostly thinking about how to make our arms touch again.

>

On the forum, I tell people I've been to twelve John Mayer concerts. I say my favorite was Atlanta because that's the closest city people would recognize. I talk about the acoustics at the Fox Theatre even though I've only seen pictures online.

> koala_rocks47: which was your favorite show of all the ones you've been to?

> Why_GeorgiaGurl: probably the one at eddie's attic. he played this unreleased song called "in your atmosphere" and everyone was dead silent

I downloaded another bootleg. Hartford, 2002. The crowd noise sounded like prayers or waves or static between radio stations.

>

I burned Drew a mix CD and almost called it "Songs for Bojangles" but at the last second I wrote "Songs for Wednesday Mornings." I included the Melbourne "Why Georgia," some Damien Rice, and other songs I thought sounded appropriately deep and romantic. Songs about longing and roads and being older than we were.

>

koala_rocks47: what's winter like there?

In Georgia, winter meant maybe putting on a fleece. Maybe frost on car windows that melted by nine a.m. In Brisbane it was summer. Upside-down seasons.

Why_GeorgiaGurl: cold sometimes

I opened a new browser and googled the distance between Brisbane and Atlanta which was 9,272 miles.

>

Drew's mix CD got scratched. The Damien Rice track skipped on "still a little bit" over and over.
"Still a little bit still a little bit still a little…"

>

That night I prayed. "Dear God, forgive me for lying about my age. And for downloading. And for the way I feel when Drew's arm touches mine during 'Comfortable.'"

>

Some girls hang out in Pastor Jim's office after school, taking photos on flip phones and listening to emo music that almost sounds like worship songs. I don't go because I don't get asked but also because when I mentioned it to my mom she furrowed her brow and said, "I don't know about that."

I rolled my eyes and told her it was perfectly fine and she said that it didn't matter. That it was a bad look.

I mentioned this to Drew, like can you believe this, and he kind of shrugged. He said, "I mean yeah, he never has the guys in his office."

>

I asked `koala_rocks47` if he believed in God and he typed for a really long time before just saying "No".

>

At Prayer Breakfast, Pastor Jim always sat next to whoever was newest. This week it was Anna from sixth grade. He asked her about her "walk with Christ" while his hand rested on her back.

My Mr. Pibb tasted flat. I couldn't finish my second biscuit. When Drew played me an unreleased Damien Rice song on the bus, I could barely pay attention to the words. I stared out the window watching the cars fly past us on Cleveland Highway and letting my mind go blank.

>

My mom asked me again about Pastor Jim and I said I hadn't noticed anything. She stared at me for a long time. I added this to my list of lies needing forgiveness.

>

koala_rocks47 messaged me less and less. Or maybe I messaged him less and less.

>

I started praying with just the beginnings. Dear God, Dear God, Dear God, Dear God, Dear God, Dear God, Dear God, Dear God—

CAVE GIRL

When my name was finally announced, 870,000 people saw the video. A voiceover—my mom's—paired with creamy, filtered clips of me in a beige onesie and tiny knit hat. I was born in October. The video was posted nine days after my birth. Three baby name experts on TikTok had predicted something similar, but not entirely accurate, about my name: that it would be vintage, cutesy. Trending but not overly popular. Perhaps something with a nature theme.

The video was shared 90,000 times and amassed close to 10,000 comments. I was a third-born, so my popularity was paved by the adorable faces of my brother and sister. My mother's bio said *Mama. Jesus follower. Homesteader.* Her feed was a sea of beige and wicker, interspersed with golden hour shots of us children frolicking in sustainably harvested linen.

Her following peaked on my first birthday with a charming video of my face covered in cake. It ended with my brother's grubby toddler hands wiping frosting from my bald head and drawing a mustache on his upper lip. Seventeen takes to achieve the illusion of spontaneity.

I wasn't allowed an iPad as a child and when all my friends got cell phones in first grade, my parents took me out of school. They fulfilled their primitive fantasy by schooling me at home. We had a blackboard and a hand-stitched chore chart. I am still so bad at math. Whatever normalcy my parents had allowed my older siblings, they'd corrected as I grew. I never watched a TV show. I wore dresses like a pilgrim.

When my sister hit me over the head with her neutral-palette building block, after being denied a second organic juice pouch, my mother's account was suspended for two weeks. The bloody gash on my forehead raised flags that became hard to explain in a simple Tik-Tok caption or Instagram story. In the aftermath, we had take-out together for the first time. Oily fried rice and crunchy, salty wontons. It was luxurious. I winced, half from pain, half from the shock of my mother's undivided attention.

On the first day of fourth-grade soccer practice, I realized my fame. I didn't have a lot of friends my age and didn't interact with people outside of my family. I was mesmerized by the soccer kids. There was a girl with beautiful red curls and big green eyes that she rolled, dramatically, when her mom grabbed my shoulder in shock. "You're [redacted]!!!" The woman squealed. I froze, as she continued to dote. "From @homesteadingmamma!" Her hand slid down my sweaty arm and I watched as the redhead's facial expression transitioned from annoyed to something closer to horrified.

When my mother was in charge of snacks, she'd pull her phone out and all the kids would run out of frame. Maybe they had NDAs to sign. PR agents to consult. Maybe their parents just told them to run. You're not ending up in the background of a @homesteadingmama sponcon post without at least getting a cut of the proceeds, Atticus. I pushed my sweaty hair out of my face and smiled. I held my free, organic granola bar in my hand proudly and propped my foot up on the soccer ball, a trained performer on a phantom stage.

Eighth grade was when all the kids started to feel nostalgic for their childhood Instagram accounts. I'd gone back to regular school, as my mother's platform had plummeted in Meta's demise. "Join me on BlackStarTM" was her last post. The platform slated to take Instagram's place crashed in the onslaught of new sign-ups, never to return. For months there was a void, and no one knew anything about anyone. We saw people at the grocery store and turned away from them, ashamed. Suddenly everyone was a luddite, just like me.

I never had an account to mourn, but I knew my mother had made an impact on the platform in the way I was received, just walking around town. "There's little [redacted]," they would say when I passed by. I was famous for learning to walk in a pristine, autumn meadow as the sun set behind me. A subject for gentle parenting lessons. A farmhouse dress and a messy free-range dinner. A bath in a big barn sink. Pixels that we thought would last forever.

"You really were the blueprint," My redheaded soccer crush told me in her bedroom that year. At 13, I'd found a way to reframe my infatuation with her into something more sustainable—a best friend. "My mom talks about it a lot," she said. "I think you're why she wouldn't let me have more than fifteen minutes of screen time."

My older sister applied to art school with a senior thesis centered around "early Instagram nostalgia". She painted photos of lattés with a thick brown haze over them. Farmer's market flowers shrouded by vignette. A salad. A puppy. Not our puppy, I'm not sure whose puppy. The crackly old film filter, which seemed even more ridiculous when she painted them in her fat, cartoonish brush strokes. My sister's teacher thought she was a genius. She got a scholarship from SCAD.

When I turned eighteen, I joined a support group for children of influencers that I learned about from a flier stapled to a telephone poll. It met once a week in a church basement, just like Alcoholics Anonymous, but it wasn't, so people brought wine.

"I'm [redacted] and I'm the daughter of an influencer," I confessed at my first meeting. A choir of tired voices sang back to me, "Hi [redacted]."

The support group was full of complete freaks, which was how I realized that I, too, was probably a complete freak. I began hanging out with a girl a few years older than me, who told me that we'd met at a brand shoot for naturally dyed hairbows when I was three. She showed me the photo of us, printed out on a piece of computer paper, after my third meeting. I could faintly see the scar on my head from the block incident.

"You were sweet," she said, "quiet…did what your mom told you to."

She printed out all her mom's content and kept it in a shoebox in her apartment. In the panicked days before the death of Instagram, when the rumors were swirling and hysteria was increasing, her mother had gone to Staples and created the hard copies.

"I hate looking through them," she told me. "But I knew this was you, the second I saw you."

My brother wrote me a letter, checking in on me, six months after I attended the first meeting. He lived a somewhat normal life. Maybe it's biological. The new data suggests that women are more affected by being the child of an influencer than men. I learned this in group. I found myself resenting him for his normalcy. I couldn't help but wonder how different I might be if I'd had those extra years of real school, those nights of mindless TV. Would I be sitting in this church basement now, or would I be out there, blissfully unaware of how the internet, and my lack of it, had shaped me?

I wrote him back and told him about group. About how we drank wine and role-played as our biggest internet troll. I told him that none of it was really helping me, mentally, but that I'd (re)met the love of my life and that she had a shoebox with a photo of me in it under her bed.

It took him weeks to respond to my letter with, "Congrats, [redacted]." Little pieces of confetti flew out of the envelope, upon opening.

My sister started making her paintings on the sides of buildings. People loved the hit of nostalgia, paired with the physicality of the place. The irony of preserving fleeting online moments on seemingly lasting structures. She got a write-up in the newspaper, paired with a photo of her in front of her latest piece—a woman's shoes surrounded by autumn leaves in the "Ludwig" filter. It was painted on the side of an old gas station. Three weeks after the article ran, they bulldozed the building. She tells me it's a Sweetgreen now.

I found it easy to be in a relationship with another ACOI (Adult Child of an Influencer). She understood my aversion to the color beige and respected my technology-free life. I never once let her take a picture of me, but she would sketch my face at the dinner table. We had a whole wall in our bedroom of just my charcoal-lined profile.

She was sixteen when the Metaverse collapsed, and she ran away from home. She lived in a commune in the North Carolina mountains where she learned to draw. She doesn't speak to her mother.

I heard from my own mother once a year in a Christmas Card-esque newsletter, forwarded from my old address, which typically showed up sometime in early January. She provided updates about herself and my siblings. She'd taken to astrology and natural medicine. Started training to be a yoga teacher.

At twenty-three, my fiancée and I got a good deal on a property and moved into a cave. We stopped receiving my mother's newsletters. The AOCI group fizzled, though there were some people who we kept in touch with through smoke signals. They seemed to be doing well.

We took to cave life effortlessly. We woke with the sun and fell asleep to the stars. My wife cooked me dinner over a fire every evening, and while the embers burned out she'd dip a stick into the charcoal. I'd lay naked for her as she traced my outline onto our thick cave walls.

We grew old together, in our cave. The figures multiplied, spanning every last inch of the walls. They tell a story—just for us—of my aging body. Of our love. Of our home.

EPILOGUE

That summer, my sister and I dug up the remains of our dead guinea pig in the backyard, wide-eyed and dumb. The shoebox that held his lifeless body was covered in tiny white maggots. We couldn't bring ourselves to remove the lid.

The dogwood trees bloomed for longer than usual that summer. There was a line of them down the hill by our house, right where the guinea pig had been buried and then re-buried. When my sister and me were down there, it was like anything could happen.

That summer, Lydia Royal died in a boat accident, and the whole fifth-grade class went to her funeral, which was open-casket, even though her head got all messed up from the motor. She wore a lavender dress.

I turned eleven that summer. An age Lydia would never reach. Me and the other girls cried and cried at our sleepovers. It seemed like we were all trying to outdo each other—see who could have the most tears, who could hold the most sadness. We'd never known anybody to die before.

That summer, I scraped my knees and booty-danced in the church gym. I watched two girls kiss to an Usher song. I tried to learn to skateboard.

I saved up all my money for a lime green camcorder that summer. I kept the bills in a shoebox under my bed, just like the one the guinea pig was resting in out back. I rode my skateboard around the neighborhood with the camera flipped open in my palm, falling and ending my footage with several seconds of the crisp, blue sky above.

That summer, a man had a heart attack behind the wheel and drove into my bedroom while I was at the grocery store with my mom and sister. When we pulled up to the house, she told me to stay in the backseat, buckled, until my grandma came to get me.

I painted my room neon green that summer. I liked how my bedroom contrasted my sister's, which was all soft pastels and porcelain dolls wedged into metal display stands. My room was my own, glowing loudly all around me.

That summer was the summer it rained every single afternoon, a slow rumble of thunder moving in at three p.m. on the dot. The asphalt would steam in the sunlight after a big storm. I tried to capture the vapor rising on my camcorder, but the lens went foggy, the same way it did when my sister got her face too close.

I bought my first Abercrombie shirt that summer. I had a crush on my friend's older brother, and we slow-danced to *All or Nothing* by O-Town at her birthday party in that same church gym. He was shorter than me and put his arms on my shoulders like the girls, while mine held his hips like a boy.

That summer, I started confirmation classes and learned about Presbyterianism and predestination. God's eternal decree. The short life of my guinea pig, Lydia Royal, and the man in the car all determined to be that length before they even made it onto this planet. It felt too big to hold.

I read *The Diary of Anne Frank* that summer. I saw *Lilo and Stitch* in theaters with a boxed snack deal of kiddie popcorn, Dr. Pepper, and a package of Dots. I called my friends on their house phones and asked each of their mothers for them.

The heat let up towards the end of that summer. The dogwood flowers had all fallen, giving way to glossy green leaves, and the storms echoed further apart. My sister and I sat outside and drank big glasses of Coke with crushed ice that my dad made by taking cubes from the tray and placing them under a paper towel, hammering them to pieces on the front steps of our home. I thought about God knowing just where each cube would break. I thought about crying.

ACKNOWLEDGEMENTS

Thank you to the publications that brought previous versions of these stories into the world: *Joyland, The Quarterless Review, Y2K Quarterly, The Nervous Breakdown, Shabby Dollhouse, XRAY Literary Magazine* and Loblolly Press's *Understory*.

Thank you to everyone who was an early reader of these stories and gave me feedback, support and love throughout the process.

Thank you to Loblolly Press and to Andrew for everything.

Thank you to Kate, I love you.

LOBLOLLY PRESS

Loblolly Press is an independent press based out of Asheville, North Carolina that is dedicated to publishing contemporary poetry, short fiction, and novels from emerging and marginalized writers across the American South. Our goal is to publish writers with a distinctly Southern voice from communities and experiences not always represented in traditional publishing. We're striving to create a community of writers and readers who feel deeply connected to the work we publish because they can see themselves represented within it.

RECENT AND FORTHCOMING FROM LOBLOLLY PRESS

The Surfacing of Joy　Earl J. Wilcox (2023)

If Lost　Clint Bowman (2024)

Distant Relations　Cheryl Whitehead (2025)

Beasts of Chase　Andrew Mack (2025)

The Computer Room　Emma Ensley (2025)

Proud Roads　Kelly Riedesel (2025)

Habitats　Garrett Ashley (2026)

Headings set in Monaco. Text set in Minion Pro.